ALAN SHIVERS

The Namaste Slasher

*Copyright © 2024 by Alan Shivers*

*All rights reserved. No part of this publication may be reproduced, stored or transmitted in any form or by any means, electronic, mechanical, photocopying, recording, scanning, or otherwise without written permission from the publisher. It is illegal to copy this book, post it to a website, or distribute it by any other means without permission.*

*This novel is entirely a work of fiction. The names, characters and incidents portrayed in it are the work of the author's imagination. Any resemblance to actual persons, living or dead, events or localities is entirely coincidental.*

*Alan Shivers asserts the moral right to be identified as the author of this work.*

*Alan Shivers has no responsibility for the persistence or accuracy of URLs for external or third-party Internet Websites referred to in this publication and does not guarantee that any content on such Websites is, or will remain, accurate or appropriate.*

*Designations used by companies to distinguish their products are often claimed as trademarks. All brand names and product names used in this book and on its cover are trade names, service marks, trademarks and registered trademarks of their respective owners. The publishers and the book are not associated with any product or vendor mentioned in this book. None of the companies referenced within the book have endorsed the book.*

*First edition*

*This book was professionally typeset on Reedsy. Find out more at reedsy.com*

*This one is for the Croatians in my life, you're all gems! Special shout-out to Martina (my Budapest buddy), Antonija (my fellow queer horror author), and Ivan (expert on all things history) for giving me a great insight into your culture & history.
Hvala!*

# Foreword

TRIGGER WARNING:

Please check for trigger warnings at the back of the book, after "About the author."

## Preface

When I finished my slasher trilogy "Europea Halls", I knew I wanted to continue in the genre, but stay fresh at the same time. It took me a good month or two before it hit me at the end of my daily meditation: how fun (and, admittedly, screwed up) would it be to write a mindfulness retreat Slasher? The moment I feel at my safest and most relaxed is during a meditation session, so the dichotomy of that feeling mixed in with terror wet my horror appetite.

Meditation and mindfulness play a key role in my life and have helped me a lot when it comes to my mental health. Writing this book, I didn't want to mock any of that. If anything, I wanted to mock *myself*, because - as the Flemish saying goes - "Self-mockery is the beginning of all wisdom."

So, have a little meditation session, burn some sage, grab your healing crystals, and scream your soul out. Are your Chakras open yet?

# Acknowledgments

The release date of "The Namaste Slasher" (October 1) marks my one year anniversary as a published author. Four books in, I'm still a newbie and I've got tons to learn. Thankfully, I've met many people along the way who have helped me shape my stories.

Thank you to all the authors that have become friends through Indie Horror Chapter in Birmingham. Meeting you people was a turning point for me, as I no longer felt isolated in my writing career. I have found my fellow weirdos!

Sarah Jules and Emerald O'Brien, my fellow Slasher Queens, you continue to inspire me. Thanks for the chats, the feedback, the tips, and for being great human beings.

To all my ARC readers and reviewers, my books would be nowhere without your support. I appreciate you all so much for spending your free time on my stories and spreading the word.

I'm glad I got to talk to so many BIPOC and Croatian Sensitivity Readers this time around. Thank you for your constructive criticism and honest feedback. I have learned a lot and I hope I'll do you all proud.

My go-to Beta reader and friend Sharron, what on earth would I do in this little horror world without you? You were my first ever reviewer and I am so happy to say we've become true friends along the way. Love you!

My editor Amanda: I'm sure I confuse you endlessly with my

'Belgian English'! Thanks for being a rock and a kind soul. To many more projects together in the future!

I'm so glad I semi-stalked "Aretheyalldead" on Instagram. He has created some genuinely stunning poster art for slasher films over the years and I was delighted when he agreed to make the cover art for my book. I have plucked your book cherry, and I hope you'll get to make many more book covers (including mine).

Jordana from PrettyKillerPodcast: thanks so much for being there when I'm doubting myself or when I need to vent about the silliest details. All of you at the PodcastCore4 are awesome people!

To anyone who has shown interest and interviewed me for their newsletters, magazines or Podcasts: I'm grateful you'd even show interest in the first place, thanks so much for promoting my books.

To the man himself, Victor Miller, screenwriter of "Friday the 13th": I still can't get over how kind and generous you've been towards me. Interviewing you has been a highlight in my slasher life so far! I hope you'll enjoy my books.

Apart from horror world, I'm a lucky man for being surrounded in my day-to-day life by people who are far more sane than I am.

My roomies Anina and Natalie: without you two - and obviously doggo Blanche - I would've been in complete isolation for weeks. Thanks for being there!

My parents, your unwavering support still means the world and I will never, ever take it for granted. Ik zie jullie graag.

To all my friends (especially Cleo, you've been with me throughout this entire ride) and family who show up and show interest, it makes my job a tad bit less lonely. I love you all.

Now, time for some slashing!

# Chapter 1

The nauseatingly warm breeze enters my apartment through the cracked open window by the balcony. It carries a musky smell, the overwhelming mix of the metropolis. It's only 11 AM and Paris is already burning. I should've known not to rent a place right underneath the roof, but it's not like I had a million options with my limited budget. July is usually unbearable in the city, but it seems to be getting worse each year. I can't wait to get out and go to Normandy, I need a climate that doesn't actually suffocate me.

The final notice is lying on the dining room table, glaring at me with discontent. Nobody warns you about the cost of chemotherapy, or the added anxiety of money worries. I am supposed to focus on my health and the rest "will be just fine," easy to say when you come from money or you can split the costs with your partner. I was barely getting by as it is, working crappy restaurant jobs and counting every single Euro. I have no one to fall back on, no one.

Perhaps making the move to Paris wasn't the healthiest of choices, in many ways. I stare out the window and take in the details of the Haussmann architecture around me to push the darkness down. The view from the balcony on the sixth floor was what pulled me in when I first visited the place. It's so easy to romanticise the dormer windows and mansard roofs when you explore the city. There's nowhere else in the world that has this type of architecture, really. So, I wanted to become part of it, and have a place of my own, with a marble fireplace. That didn't exactly happen, seeing as I live on the old servants' floor, where the details are far less refined and the ceilings are way lower than on the other floors. Still, a part of me felt like I had made it, living in the capital and leaving a life of heartbreak behind. Little did I know the actual pain was still ahead of me.

*Oh crap*, it's almost time. I pull the largest pillow of my velour sofa from its nook and position it on the floorboard in the living room/kitchen/bedroom. The laptop is already set up and the meeting should start any minute now. I grab a hairband from my wrist and tie my blue locks into a bun. It's what I always do when I need to focus. This Zoom call couldn't have come at a better time, I'm in dire need of relaxation. I first discovered these free meditation sessions when I started following Vera - the organiser - on Instagram. She is a hypnotherapist from Brussels, but as her private online sessions are obviously too pricey for me, I was thrilled to learn she offers free group meditation sessions once a week on Zoom. I fluff up my oversized T-shirt and sit down cross-legged on the pillow; it's time to get cosy. I suppose I was wrong to say there's no one. Vera has become my surrogate family.

The moment Vera lets me into the meeting, I spot a couple of familiar faces. I've never spoken to any of them, but somehow it makes me feel more comfortable knowing they're here. There are sixteen of us today, mostly older women. I'm probably the youngest at thirty-six. I chuckle as I notice one woman

## CHAPTER 1

has her webcam upside down and another has the cringiest background of a field of roses with a photoshopped rainbow behind it. Nobody has the cat filter on this time. Disappointing.

"Hello, my lovely people!" Vera starts off. "I'm so glad you've all decided to join me today." She has the widest grin on her face, her eyes are beaming with joy and excitement. I wish I had this woman's energy levels. I immediately feel safe.

"As you can probably tell, I'm not in my house in Brussels today. I'm taking part in a mindfulness retreat in Croatia." She moves her camera and shows us the view of the chalky colourful mountain and the beach in the far background. Fine, rub it in, will you? A couple of enthusiastic "*oohs*" and "*aahs*" jump off the screen. These women are definitely more vocal than I am in a group setting. "I start the retreat tomorrow, but I wanted to make sure I could take the time to have our session first. So, thank you all for being flexible and joining me on a Thursday." Well, this is literally the only thing on my agenda all week, so: you're welcome.

I glare at the envelope again. Over four thousand fucking Euros, how will I ever be able to pay that off? *Not now, Eloise, you deserve a break.*

"Right, people, why don't we start with a little body scan?"

Vera guides us, and we gradually move from the top of our crown down to our toes, whilst always focusing on the breath. I can tell that almost my entire body is cramped up from the stress I've been holding in. I try to breathe through the tension and allow myself to soften. It's not working as well as I'd like, but I do notice a first hint of relief by the time we reach the toes about fifteen minutes in. Just when I am at the point of letting go, a loud barking sound emanates from one of the participants' microphones. I immediately tense back up and open my eyes in confusion. A Golden Retriever's wet nose is filling up one of the screens.

"Oh my, I'm ever so sorry!" One of the older ladies says. "Pippa! Pippa, down girl!" The dog starts frantically licking the woman's face. We all burst out laughing, even though I must admit I am a tad bit annoyed. I was almost relaxed. *Damn you, Pippa.*

Vera smiles gently. "That's okay, Veronique. I would kindly ask you all to make sure your microphones are muted." Bless her, she has to remind the group at least three times every session. I wouldn't have her patience, no way. I double-check mine, yup - the mic's off.

"Is it off?" Another lady yells.

"Eh, no darling. We can hear you." A tiny crack flickers in Vera's smile.

"Oh, right. This technology, I swear - it does my head in. Hold on - how about now?"

"Still - we can still hear you, Linda. It's the tiny button on the bottom of the screen."

"The one that looks like a microphone?"

"That's the one, yes." That smile is holding on for dear life.

"I can't - I swear I had it last time. Barry!" Oh lord, this again. A tiny bald man walks up to the screen. Looks like he already knows what the question will be. "Barry, love, the mic, I can't seem to switch it off." The man bites his lips and immediately turns off the microphone. Linda shows us an apologetic two thumbs up.

Vera's lips look a bit tense now. "Okay, thank you, Barry. We can use these little hiccoughs as mindfulness moments. Things won't always go the way we want them to, there will be distractions in life, but we can utilise them as a practice to go back to our breathing. Always bring it back to the breathing." She slowly exhales and loosens up her facial muscles. I try to follow suit.

"Now that we are all set, I will move into the core meditation of the day. Today we will focus even more on breath work, so I welcome you all to close your eyes." I do so; this is my favourite part of the session. "Shake off any tension that might reside in your shoulders and let them droop down. Keep your eyes closed until again I ask you to open them. If any noises happen to occur around you, that is absolutely fine. We can never guarantee complete silence in everyday life. If you get distracted or lose yourself in thought, be kind to yourself and bring it back to your breathing self. Now, let's start by inhaling to the count of four, holding the breath for two seconds, and exhaling to the count of six."

We do this for a couple of rounds, followed by the sound of Vera's gradually quieting voice and a faint backing track of nature sounds she has put on. I turn inwards, the way I only can when guided by her. It starts with a black canvas. Then the colours splash off in all directions, twirling shapes converge and diverge across the spectrum of my mind. I dive into this deep state of trance where nothing makes sense but, then again, it shouldn't anyway. It's all about loosening up and following the breath. I usually give the inhale one particular colour and the exhale another one. If I'm feeling especially positive, the inhale tends to be orange. When I am in need of purifying, I go for light pink instead. I try to follow the path of the inhale as it fills up my body. The exhale is always dark grey. Exhale the cancer, the toxins, the past that followed me to Paris, everything that has been causing grief. Some sessions the grey gets a little darker, it depends on my mental state.

I notice a tiny teardrop gliding off my cheek. *That's fine, don't judge it. Be kind to yourself.* I check if the Cordierite guiding stone is in my right pocket. It is, good. I let my fingers glide across its smooth surface. Somehow my chest opens up a bit more and a rush of tears flows down. I instantly feel better. Keeping all the stress to yourself when going through this process is too much for anyone to handle. I wish I had family or a partner to turn to, but it's just me and the city. We enter the final part of the session in which the backing track continues. Vera gives us about ten minutes to go even deeper inwards without her guidance, so it's just our breathing and the sounds of nature.

My doorbell rings.

I jolt out of the colours, into the now and instinctively check if my microphone is definitely turned off. I squint at the screen - it's still muted, good. Horrible timing, I bet it's my crystals that should've arrived over a week ago. I buzz the intercom and recognise the voice of the postman. See, I knew it. I can pick it up after the session, I don't want to lose out on too much.

I turn around and head back towards the pillow. Everyone's eyes are still closed, lucky bastards. I want to go back to the headspace they're at.

My chest tightens back up.

Something's off.

I frown and focus on the screen to make sure I'm not losing my mind.

A man is standing behind Vera.

He's wearing some deformed Buddha mask and a long, black raggedy cloak.

Is this supposed to be - what *is* this? Vera's eyes are still closed. She must feel the man's presence, this is probably part of the session, *right?* She is at this retreat, maybe he works there. I'm sure the guy will walk off in a second, he must've entered the wrong room.

Then why is my jaw locked tight? Should I unmute and scream at her?

I'm frozen, waiting for a signal.

The man moves closer to Vera. His steps are calculated and confident. It doesn't look like he's leaving that room.

A rusty saw slips out of one of his sleeves. My stomach clenches up. This can't be real.

That's it. I run towards the laptop, but accidentally kick it further down the room. *Fuck. Clumsy fuck.*

Tingles run down my left arm. How is nobody else seeing this?

I rush to the laptop, careful not to kick it this time.

The masked man is standing right behind Vera. She's still deep in her meditative state. So are all the others.

I duck down and press unmute.

"Vera! Vera, behind you!" My voice is hoarse and shaky.

Vera opens her eyes, along with the rest of the group. Everyone sees the mask.

A muted symphony of screams fills the meeting.

Before Vera can turn around, the man puts the saw in front of her throat and starts cutting into her. She cries for help, the gurgling sounds too awful to register. Maroon drops splash all over her camera screen. I grab my own throat, it's as if I can't breathe. What can I do? How can I help?

Two people leave the meeting. Linda grabs her phone and films everything. Good, evidence, smart thinking.

I want to look away, but I can't. More blood spurts out as

minute pieces of the torn pink skin of her neck flop down onto the ground. The man grabs Vera's hair to pull her head back - exposing her neck - and saws even deeper. Her eyes roll up whilst her head starts shaking.

I can't look at her, so I study the mask.

It's an off-white mask of Siddharta, burnt on one side.

One final cut.

The hair-raising yelps stop. This can't actually be happening. There's no way.

The masked killer holds onto Vera's decapitated head as he pushes the rest of her body down to the floor. The fleshy strings of her neck carry the blood to the ground. The disgust and utter shock in the other people's faces tell me this *is* real. More people leave the meeting. In fact, everyone does. I guess they don't want to be recognised.

*Not Vera, not the one person who's been there.*

The mask stares into my eyes. He doesn't move. It's just him and me.

I need to go, but something is blocking me from leaving. Once I leave, it'll be just me. She'll be gone. I won't have anyone to go back to. A quick scan of my screen reminds me I didn't put my actual name down for the sessions. The killer doesn't know my real name is Eloise.

The mask comes closer to the bloodied screen.

I try to breathe in, but my chest is locked.

Then a window pops up.

"The organiser has finished the meeting."

## Chapter 2

3 YEARS LATER

I wish I would've driven here. I hadn't taken a plane in years, what with the entire cancer treatment. For some reason the smallest things scare me nowadays, I thought it'd be the opposite. I battled through months of pain, with the occasional - not so minor - bumps on the road, but I made it to remission. To my absolute surprise, a neighbour from the building had set up a GoFundMe campaign when she spotted me crying on the staircase. I'm not normally the one to ask for help, but I had nothing left in me. I was broke and sick. The crowdfunding worked so well that I had some money left after the treatment, so I decided to pamper myself with a trip. I hadn't actually ever left France since I moved there. I didn't particularly feel the need to. However, I genuinely think I deserve a break from Paris. Routines can become equally - if not more - suffocating as the climate of that city. So, here I am, on my first-ever retreat. This isn't exactly a cheap one either. I hope I won't be surrounded by rich obnoxious twats.

   You hear these stories about cancer survivors who are soaking it all up - living their best lives and all that shit, but that's not the case for me. Planes, roller coasters, crowded places -

they all frighten me now. They never used to. Taking a plane on my own for the first time in forever was a big one. I'm still a bit wobbly in the knees, but I'm also proud of myself. It's a good thing the flight from Paris to Zagreb only takes two and a half hours. It flew by. Oh lord, dad joke - forgive me. That's what happens when you're almost forty.

I'm scanning the crowd in the massive arrival hall for someone with a plate that has my name on it. I'm supposed to be picked up here. There are so many taxi drivers with signs though; guess I unlocked another fear: not finding my name at an airport. The chaos and noises around me certainly don't help either. People's voices bounce off the high ceilings, sending muffled echoes into my eardrums. I quickly tie up my locks. My palate is dry, I could do with a drink. I'm starting to get sweaty, *why* did you go for two layers, Elo?

A tall older man - I'm guessing he's in his late sixties or early seventies - wearing a small straw hat - walks up to me. There's something stoic about him, so I catch myself taking a hesitant step backward.

"Miss LaCroix?"

Oh, right, now it makes sense. I wasn't looking for a plate with *two* names on it. "Yes, that's me, thanks! You can call me Eloise, mister -?"

"Milo. No mister, just Milo." A forced smile appears on his leathery face. *Right*, now it clicks. I saw this guy in the ad for the retreat. At least he speaks a bit of English, that's a good start. That wouldn't often happen with older people in Paris, let's be honest. I glance at the other name on the plate and a flashback of my Dutch classes back in Curacao hits me - I was never the best at pronunciation. Milo stretches out his arm and waves at a young blonde girl. His eyes open widely.

## CHAPTER 2

"Miss Vankampenhouten!" I see how it is. Put a pretty little thing in front of him and the enthusiasm is dialed up a couple of notches. How refreshing.

The girl frowns first - even *I* could tell Milo completely butchered her name -, then smiles back at him and replies: "That's me! Are you part of Zelena Nada?"

"Yes, I am. This lady here -" Lady? I'm not ancient, you twat. "Is also coming."

The girl throws me a warm look and goes in straight for a hug and a kiss. I lean in for the second kiss, but she stops right before I reach her other cheek.

"One kiss?" I ask awkwardly. "Let me guess: you're Belgian!"

"How did you know?"

"Your name. We're neighbours. I'm French." A part of me wants to speak Dutch to her, but I'm not here to live in the past.

"Oh, great! Sorry, I should've given you two more then. Here!" She goes in for two more pecks and gives my arm a cute little squeeze. "By the way, love the red locks, girl. It's giving!"

Oh, they've accepted Gen Zs on the mindfulness retreat too, it seems. She's obviously a bit younger. Then again, I can't really tell how old she is. She's definitely had some work done on her lips and cheeks - no shade, just saying it as it is - so it's hard to tell. I bet my money she's wearing hair extensions too. It's exactly as I feared: rich people.

"The name's Aagje." She continues. "And you are?"

"Eloise. You can call me Elo though." Milo looks slightly offended that I didn't give him the same permission.

She seems kind enough. I'm a bit rusty at the whole meeting-new-people thing. It's been years of isolation and solitude. If

I'm being honest, I have grown a bit bitter and wary of the world. I want to give this one a chance, I'm not exactly swimming in a pool of friendships. I push aside my slight annoyance at how ditsy and chipper she sounds. At least she's friendly to me, I'll take that.

We all get into a dusty black van that has certainly seen better days, but it beats taking two trains to get to our destination.

"So, what's the name again of the place we're going to?" Aagje wonders, leaning over to the left at the back of the van, so she can see Milo better.

"You say before. Name is Zelena Nada. Means 'Green Hope' in English."

"No - no, I meant: what's the name of the area, or the town?"

Milo nods, showing her that he gets it now. "Ah, yes. Name of place is Velebit. It is like a big -" He gestures some sort of a large bump.

"A mountain?" Aagje fills in.

"Yes, mountain Velebit. Is in area Trnovac."

Aagje pokes me and giggles. "These Croatian names, they're not the easiest to pronounce, are they?"

I giggle back out of sheer stress response before I realise I sound like a constipated schoolgirl. "No, they're not. I like the language though."

"Oh my God, same! Slavic languages are so - *mysterious*." She puts on a dead serious face. "Like, it's giving *powerful*." I hope she won't drag out her adjectives like that the entire trip.

"It sure is giving something."

"Right?" She tilts her head back at Milo. "Sir -"

"Is Milo." He smiles and winks at her. Gross.

"Milo, sorry. How long does it take to get to Velebit?"

## CHAPTER 2

He looks confused so I try to simplify the question. "One hour, two hours?"

That works. "Oh, yes. Two hours and half." My heart sinks into my shoes. That's a long ass ride to be seated next to 'it's giving drama'. I shake my head and exhale slowly. Don't be like this. You didn't get to this point in life to be prejudiced about a girl who is just being friendly. Give her a shot. A *proper* one.

"So, Aagje. Am I saying that right?"

The giggle is back. "Almost. The "g" sound is a tricky one in Flemish, but you're better than most French people." That's because once, in a previous life, I spoke your language, girl.

"Thanks. What brings you here?" Great, could I make it sound any more like a job interview?

"Oh, girl, many things. Where do I even start?" Oh lord, please let this be a short answer. "I suppose I need to find myself in life. I got lost along the way."

Cryptic, but I'll take it. At least it was a short -

"Actually, let me try to word that better." Superb. "I'm an influencer and brand ambassador for an organic cosmetics company from Norway. Maybe you've heard of them, they're called Ösmö." Ah, there we have it. An influencer. "I was sent here on a sponsorship deal. I'll have to film the occasional reels and all that - but at the end of the day, I'm really here for myself. Like, finding out what's underneath it all."

"Underneath? The make-up?"

"Ha, you're a witty one!" Another poke. "No, like this rat race of a society we live in. I'm only twenty-three and I've had three burnouts. That's not normal, is it?"

"It - no, it really isn't."

"*Right*? So, I hope I get a better understanding of who I truly am and what makes me tick." I'm not sure how to reply. She looks a bit disappointed. Oh crap, she expected an answer from me. She probably wanted something savvy, me being the older woman. Brain fart.

"So, how about you, Elo? What brings you here?" She winks, bouncing back my oddly put question.

What brings me here? Do I give her the truth, the half-truth, or some made-up shit?

I glare outside the dusty window and take in the glorious mountains and turquoise waters. The breeze here is warm too, but it feels healthier. I'm not stuck in a concrete jungle anymore. This is a new place. A chance for a do-over.

"I'm in remission from cancer. I-"

"Oh, girl, I'm so sorry! If I may ask - and if I'm being too blunt, please tell me - what type?"

"Breast." I touch the silicone on the left side. "This one. It had to be taken out." I surprise myself with how emotional it makes me. My eyes are watery. Aagje pulls my right hand in her lap. "You're so brave for being so open. So *authentic*." Why is she annoying me, when she's actually right?

"Thanks."

"No, I really mean that." She stares deep into my eyes. It makes me a bit uneasy.

"Okay, I appreciate that. Anyway, ever since I was diagnosed I have been on the search for - how do I put this? For what this is all about. You know, the purpose. So I got into spirituality for the first time in my life. Things like meditation, healing stones -"

"Yes, Elo, totally! Same!" She erupts with enthusiasm and shows me her Black Obsidian gem. "To cleanse my aura." She adds. I have to give it to her, she's right about its function.

## CHAPTER 2

"Sorry, I interrupted you. So, what do you hope to find here?"

"Peace of mind, I suppose would be an honest reply. A way of coping with the grief."

And answers. But Aagje doesn't need to know that. Why was Vera killed on this retreat? Why didn't anyone uncover the truth behind her murder? I might be here to find peace of mind, but I'm sure as hell not leaving until I know who killed Vera. It's a funny one, that. So many things scare me, but this doesn't. This one is about justice. I got to live through my chemo while the only person that helped me cope was butchered in front of my eyes.

*That's* why I am here. To take off that mask.

## Chapter 3

The last twenty minutes or so of the ride are spent in silence. I think she noticed my social battery was running on empty. It's all still new to me, opening up to people. I'm grateful she's given me some space. Maybe she's more empathetic than I had given her credit for. Something about her young enthusiasm annoyed me so much that I'm sure it has more to do with me than her. It's a shame I only recognise these things after they happen. I want to do better; for the people around me, but also myself. So here we are, both staring out of the windows, taking in the stunning scenery around us. We're driving on rough sand roads now, with sharp U-turns leading us higher towards the mountain summit. The turquoise waters float further and further away. I hope we'll get a chance to go for a dip, but it looks quite far already from here and we haven't even arrived yet. The higher up the mountain we get, the more desolate everything looks. Earlier on we passed some quaint towns, but most of the houses on the mountains look abandoned. The absence of people is not new to me, but somehow these derelict buildings alarm me. Something is unsettling about the way the facades glare back.

So, you probably wonder what happened after Vera was killed.

## CHAPTER 3

Not that much is the sad truth. Linda was questioned the most, seeing as she sent the video footage to the Croatian police. I was only questioned twice by them. Over a Zoom call, which was fun - triggers, anyone? The first time they asked rather general questions about how it all went down. I can't even recall most of their questions. The second time, though, they needed details. They asked about the room she was in, and if I remembered anything specific. I didn't, except for the view. It seems like the police were trying to figure out where it happened - which is odd, as she was registered for the mindfulness retreat and surely the organisers must've known where she went to hold our session. Then again, maybe she just used whatever room was available at the last minute. The retreat hadn't started yet and I don't remember seeing a bed in the background, so it might not have been her bedroom. There was one question I *could* help them with though.

"Could you describe the mask to us, please?"

I could. That mask is engraved into my memory and my nightmares. An off-white Siddharta mask, with the right side being darker - dirtier. That side looked slightly burnt to a muddy brown colour, as if the killer had been through some fights in the past. That part of the mask reminded me of a droopy, melted candle. The features were all off.

As it turned out, Vera *had* gone to a different room, the 'sound bowl healing room'. Other than that, the questioning didn't lead to much. Nobody in the team at the retreat had heard or seen anything, because most of them were off getting groceries in a nearby town. There were several searches set up by the local police and the retreat was shut down immediately. But they didn't catch whoever did this to Vera.

I *know*, rationally at least, that going there the summer they open back up is a dumb idea. But something still pulled me, some sort of gravity I couldn't control. I need answers, perhaps to get closure and to find a way to move on. If this killer is still on a spree, Zelena Nada is the place he'd go, right? Unless, of course, the police being on the lookout for him has led him to change his hunting grounds. I admit, it's not the smartest idea. However, there's no rationale involved when it comes to trauma. I've learned that the hard way. My brain has taught itself to be alert wherever I go - and I haven't actually gone places at all except for the necessary groceries and hospital appointments. I've seen that mask everywhere, from the corner of my eyes. In the dark, gloomy metro, in the hospital lifts, in the staircase of my apartment. He's omnipresent. That's exactly why I need closure. I've been given a new lease on life, but that part is clouding my present. I think I deserve a full chance at happiness. So here I am.

"Welcome to Zelena Nada!" Milo shouts out as we arrive at the gates. I snap out of it. I didn't expect such a high-tech electric gate with fences and barbed wire all around. I don't remember seeing that on their socials. Maybe this is their way of ensuring safety. It sure as hell doesn't *feel* safe. When you think of a mindfulness retreat the last thing I'd imagine is barbed wire.

As the gates slowly open, a tall, lanky woman with a buzz cut and a colourful floaty kimono spreads her arms wide open. Some feathery earrings that look like tiny dream catchers flutter in the summer air. Aagje and I step out of the van and walk towards her. Milo stays behind and opens the trunk to take care of our luggage. The woman gives Aagje a tight hug - as if they've known each other for years - and panic sets in when I realise I'm next. Right before she comes in for a hug, her eyes startle me. They're gorgeous, yet almost alienesque. Actually no, they remind me of Husky's eyes. Light blue, almost white, with a distinctly dark circle around them. *Be still, my heart.* She can do a lot more to me than just hugging. I wink at her - oh for fuck's sake, did you need to embarrass yourself the first second? - and enjoy the embrace. Two hugs in one day so far. More than I've had in the last three years. I hold back the unexpected tears that are welling up, my body aching for more affection. I hadn't allowed myself to miss physical touch, but now that I've had a taste of it, I don't want to let go.

"Well, aren't you a magnificently gorgeous pair? Welcome! My name is Xen."

"Zen?" Aagje asks politely.

"No, Xen. With an X, darling. My pronouns are 'she' and 'they'. Whatever feels right for you."

"Thanks for the lovely reception, Xen. My pronouns are 'she/her' and my name is Aagje and -"

"Oh, the promo winner! It's an absolute delight to have you." The two seem to be clicking already.

"And - and my name's Eloise. Or Elo, as you wish."

Awkward silence, what did I do wrong?

"And your pronouns -?"

Oh, right. That's still fairly new to me. "Are she/her." More silence. "And I love the 'shes'." I smile, hoping Xen will catch on. "I'm a lesbian." I add. I would love for someone to install a word vom filter inside my brain right here, right now. *I'm* not desperate, *you* are.

"Okay. Well, welcome Elo. Everyone is welcome at Zelena Nada!" They're not telling me if they're queer too? Oh, come on. "Will you girls follow me to the main hall? I'll introduce you to the rest."

"Everyone's already here?" Aagje walks a bit in front of me, playing the role of teacher's pet.

"I believe so. There were supposed to be two more people, Arnaud and Erik, a couple from Belgium - but I never heard back from them."

Great, another thing that petrifies me: arriving last in a group setting. I usually get somewhere well ahead of time, so that I can nestle in a corner seat. Either that, or scan the room for a dog and stay put. This is all about getting out of that comfort zone though. Not much left of that zone by the time this day's finished, I'm afraid. I feel exhausted already, my energy levels sure aren't anywhere near my pre-cancer days.

I've got this. They're just people. I pull my bun a little tighter.

## Chapter 4

I try to take in as many of the details as I can before heading into the main building of the lot. There's a hint of faded beauty regarding the Roman columns and the typical triangular pediment. I once read that parts of Croatia - like Pula - were part of the Roman empire and that the country has an interesting mix of historical elements in its architecture, even down to the city planning. I suppose this building is part of that past, even though it looks more like a tacky pastiche than an actual Roman temple. The faded pink and baby blue tones show that the facade has seen better days. When we enter the main atrium adorned with (I presume) Croatian landscape paintings and white marble statues, I spot the rest of the group. A sigh of relief escapes my lips when I count the heads. There's definitely not as many people here as I had feared. Except for Xen, Aagje and myself, there's only three more people. I hope that's it, I'm fine with this number.

"Come with me, girls, the rest of our group is right over there." They pinch me and give me a quick wink. They *winked*, I might still have some game after all. Aagje yet again walks a bit faster than me, so she reaches the others first. I smile, a non-sarcastic smile for the first time in a while, to see her look so happy. It reminds me of my twenty-something self when I was still living in Curacao and making new friends every other weekend at some beach party.

I make my rounds and give two guys and a girl a hug and a kiss, because I don't want to be that awkward fool who gives three French kisses after Aagje has given *one* kiss. The first victim of my calculated greeting is a slender, yet toned tall guy with blond long locks, a short beard, and piercing blue eyes. "Hello there, my name's Nils. I like the locks, sister!"

*Ooh*, they're testing me here. I bite my tongue to the point where I can almost taste blood dripping down my throat - pushing away his blatant ignorance - and smile back: "Thanks - *brother*. I'm Elo."

"Elo, cool! Is that an African name?" *Is yours a Colonial one?*

"No, it's French."

"Oh, how exotic. Where are you from, then?"

"Well, France. I live in Paris."

"I know, but I mean where are you *really* from?"

"Still Paris."

His cheeks are turning slightly red now. I can't lie, I'm enjoying this.

"Oh - yes, I mean - like, your roots?"

"Curacao. Afro-Caribbean roots." Take a deep breath. He's young. "How about you?"

"I'm Swedish." Checks out. "From a city called Göteborg."

"Don't think I've heard of that one. I've been to Stockholm, but not there."

"It's kind of the more alternative, underground capital of Sweden. It's got quite a big artistic scene." If he pulls out a Ukulele now, I'm bolting. "But it's also produced mainstream acts, like Ace of Base."

"Oh, I know them! I used to sing "All That She Wants" all

the time with my friends."

To my surprise he starts singing the chorus to the song, maybe 90s songs are the exact amount of hip again. He stops mid sentence, a look of shame in his eyes. So he *does* get it.

"Look, I'm sorry, Elo. I know how I sounded. Like an absolute white privileged douchebag." That takes me aback.

"I appreciate the apology. Let's start over." I shake his hand. "I'm Elo, nice to meet you." The gratitude practically drips off his face. No wonder I have no friends left, it's like I *want* to see fault in other people before even giving them a chance. I mean, the dude dug himself a grave from the get-go, but I don't think any of it was malicious. Dumb? Sure. Ignorant? Fuck yes. But still, that doesn't mean I need to react harshly. There's witty and then there's snarky - and I'm afraid the last few years have pulled me more towards the latter. I mean, those locks, no - just no. But apologising in front of everyone takes guts.

The next guy who goes in for an almost painfully strong hug - the dude is ripped like a Hemsworth brother - has short, light brown hair. I'm at least twenty centimetres taller than him. We love a short king.

"Elo, right?"

"Yep, that's me!"

"My name is Dimitar, or Dimi in short. I'm Bulgarian." His low baritone voice carries, and he has a bit of a military vibe about him. I suspect he is about my age or a bit older. The tight white tank top he has on is definitely there to show off how ripped he is, but somehow I doubt I'm his audience. I spotted the way he was eyeing up Nils straight away.

The last person in the group I meet is a young auburn-haired girl. She definitely has the BoBo - Bohemian Bourgeois for those not in the know - look: that wavy long hair, the white linen dress, sandals. Fashion is subjective and I'm not here to judge. Let's call it an observation. I probably look so boring to her, with my oversized T-shirt and short shorts.

"Hey there, I'm Esma!" The youthful enthusiasm of Aagje multiplied, those two will probably hit it off. She must be the youngest here. "I'm Bosnian, from right across the border. I have Croatian family too, though."

There's something refreshing about how open young people are. There's no sense of trepidation yet.

We all stand in a circle, taking in the lovely ceiling with frescoes of what looks like pagan gods of some sort.

"You might wonder why there are only five of you. The honest answer is that we were very picky in the selection process." Plus the fact that it's a crazy expensive retreat, maybe? No? "We went for the ones that we truly believe need it the most. All of you have written us a letter as to why you were interested and what made you start your spiritual path. Your stories are incredible and highly moving. You're all survivors in your own way." Guess I'm not the only one who has been through stuff here. "Next to that, you all have *some* experience with mindfulness, but you're still quite new at this. I believe I can get you all to the level that works best for you as individuals. Having big groups would take away from that. I'm so delighted to have you all here! There's something about this place, Mount Velebit, that's, how can I put it? *Magical*." They seem moved by their own words. "Well then, now that you've all met, I will show Aagje and Eloise to their tents, so they can freshen up or have a little power nap." Xen says. "I'd like everyone to be back here at seven thirty sharp, so we can have a brief tour of the premises followed by our first dinner together."

## CHAPTER 4

Xen takes Aagje and I back outside, towards our separate tents. They're about a ten minute walk from the main building, and I like the fact that they're set up underneath these thick trees. It's probably nice and cool inside. I hate waking up in an overheated tent, it reminds me too much of festival summers with horrible hangovers.

"Go ahead, have a little peek inside and I will see you in about an hour. The showers and toilets are right behind the trees opposite us. If anything is up, you've got my number - although I do try to follow through on my digital detox. I can make an exception on day one, I suppose." Another wink, I swear I'm not imagining it. It was directed at me, they weren't even close to looking at Aagje. These cobwebs might get a clean-up after all.

I unzip the tent and look around my temporary home away from home. We were promised Glamping, but I'm not too sure what's glamorous about a thin as fuck mattress and a tiny night stand. To be fair, it's definitely spacious for one person, but there's almost nothing inside. I guess they went for Scandinavian minimalism. Positive thinking, the customised towels and slippers are cute. The bouquet of pastel-coloured dried flowers also adds a homey touch. At least I was right about one thing: it's nice and fresh inside.

As I lay my head down against the fluffy pillow, I wonder where the next couple of days will take me. In the whirlwind of meeting new people I had almost forgotten about that Buddha mask.

Almost.

## Chapter 5

*Crap, crap, crap.* I should've set an alarm. I'm just ten minutes late, so I hope I won't have pissed off Xen. I want them to like me. I rush out of the tent after putting on some deodorant and sprint off to the atrium. The rest of the group is already there. Serves me right for not respecting their timing.

"I'm so sorry, I dozed off and forgot about the time!" I say, out of breath.

Xen doesn't seem perturbed at all. "That's alright, lovely. We're not here to judge one another. I'm glad the group is complete." The others give me a little wave or smile. An entire group of friendly faces, it's almost unnerving.

"Alright then, time for the grand tour!"

Xen explains the meaning behind the landscape paintings in the main hall, all referring to different areas in Croatia. One painting looks exactly like the background in Vera's meeting. I look at it a little longer than the others, hoping to find some kind of a clue. Nothing.

We walk through a rustic wooden door into a smaller room.

"This is where we will have our meditation sessions, the group part. You will all have designated slots for your solo practice too. You can choose whichever location calls to you

## CHAPTER 5

the most, but I do kindly ask that you are there alone. Solitude is an important part of the retreat too." The walls are decorated with Croatian rugs, bearing repetitive patterns of dark reds and blacks. I've seen these types of Slavic shapes before, something about it has always intrigued me. How forms and symbols can be so different, even though we're still in the same continent; it baffles me. The wooden floorboards are covered with thick yoga mats. The place oozes comfort and calmness. It's cooler here than in the other rooms so far. I'm looking forward to these sessions. I read online that we'll practice over ten different types of meditation, there's still so much to learn.

"If you follow me, I'll take you to the first floor." We head up a bombastic pink marble staircase, one you'd see in Parisian villas too. It twirls up to the next floor in a semicircle, I love the elegance of the shape. It's definitely an eclectic place, a mix of styles and colours. The landing is filled with more statues.

"Xen, what do these statues represent?" I surprise myself, usually I'm not the one to ask questions in group settings, but something about the energy of these people feels safe. Aagje locks eyes with me and smiles approvingly.

"Good question, Eloise. The collection you can find here are replicas of famous Croatian statues. It's a bit of a mishmash really. This one here is called Apoxyomenos." They point to the sculpture of a man who is cleaning himself. "The real statue is actually rather large, almost two metres tall and made out of bronze instead of white plaster. It was a statue found in the sea near the islet of Vele Orjule. A rare example of a preserved Greek statue. Further down the hall we have the statue of bishop Grgur Ninski, which can be found in -"

"Split." Esma replies proudly.

"Well done, Esma! How did you know?"

"We *are* neighbours. I still have some family living in Croatia, both here and around Split. I remember seeing that statue on Insta. It's quite impressive, isn't it like ten metres high?"

"Eight and a half I believe, but indeed - a mastodon of a structure."

"People rub his toe for good luck, if I remember correctly?"

Xen rolls their eyes, it's the first time I spot a different energy from them. "Tourists are rubbing any statue they can nowadays for good luck." They take a beat. "Anyhow, on the other side of the landing we have some other religious statues like "Our Lady of Loretto". If you have some time after the retreat, you should really explore the country. I can give you all the recommendations you need." Positive Xen is back.

"What about Communist statues?" Nils chimes in.

"What about them, darling?"

"Most of these statues look Greek, Roman or religious - I'm guessing Catholic."

"You are right. Let's just say that we have no need for Communist reminders in a place of wellness." That shuts down any further probing from mister inappropriate remarks. In his own words, he's still learning. Nils purses his lips in an attempt to ask a follow-up question, but miraculously holds it in when he looks at me. I'm not exactly subtle when it comes to showing emotions. I guess my frown did its job.

"The first door on the left leads us to the 'sound healing room,' which is where we will hold our sound baths." I freeze for a moment before stepping into the room. This is where Vera was killed. This exact room.

I sense an invisible hand around my throat, making it hard to swallow. Three years have passed, but I can still recognise that view of the sea through the windows at the back of the room.

CHAPTER 5

A mix of small, medium-sized and large copper sound bowls are spread throughout the room. It has all the right elements to make one be at peace, from the soft colours on the walls to the plethora of small rugs laid out nonchalantly on the floor. The room can't fool me though. I know what happened here. I wonder if Xen does too. We'll see how things evolve. Let's hope for a moment between them and I where I can ask about - you know, Vera.

"Are you alright, Elo?" Aagje gently strokes my arm. "You look lost."

I turn my head towards her. I was right about the empathy levels with this girl. "I'm fine. Thanks though." I whisper back. I want to make sure the others don't hear me, but to my relief they're talking to Xen about the schedule of the day.

"Are you sure? If you have anxiety issues I can lend you my lavender roll." She takes out a tiny balm. "Just put a bit on your wrists and it'll calm you right down."

I would usually refuse any kind of help, but I promised myself to be open. "Thanks so much, I'll try it." I roll the balm over my left wrist and have a smell. It's lush. Aagje nods. "Told you it works. Have a slow inhale and let it do its thing." She puts her hand on my back. "I'm here for you. I don't know what you've been through, I can only imagine what cancer does to a person, but you've made it here and you're not alone." Damn, she knows how to hit them feels. A tear rolls down my cheek, I quickly brush it off with my hand and get another hit of the lavender smell. The others turn around and face me too. Oh no, not the pity party please.

"Are you alright?" Nils asks in a surprisingly kind manner.

"I'll be fine, sorry." My voice is barely audible, my throat still feeling closed up.

"Don't apologise for being real, sis." He shoots me a little coy glance.

"Thanks, bro." I reply, a small laugh breaking through the hurt.

After some consoling from the entire group - I swear it was *not* my intention to draw the attention to me - Xen shows us the kitchen on the first floor. A bit of an odd set-up, not having a kitchen on the ground floor.

"We will have our meals outside whenever possible, and it seems like the weather gods are with us for the duration of our retreat. So, are we feeling peckish?" Xen wonders.

More like starving. Everyone replies in unison, like a group of school kids on a trip who are about to be fed their stale sandwiches.

"Then let's head back out and meet Josip, our cook. As you know, all meals will be fully vegetarian and -"

"There are vegan options too, right?" Dimitar asks, a hint of worry in his voice.

"Oh, absolutely! You have all filled in your dietary requirement, and we take health very seriously here - both mental and physical well-being are our top priority."

"Thanks so much." He replies. That voice of his is so deep that even the kindest of words come out sounding a bit menacing. But looking at the guy, I can tell he's such a teddy bear. A muscled one at that, sure, but his eyes exude pure kindness.

"My pleasure, love. We also have plenty of gluten-free options for Aagje and Esma or whoever feels like mixing it up a bit. So, without further ado, let's eat!"

## Chapter 6

As we head outside, I spot Milo next to a large banquet rich in colours and textures awaiting us. The cook beams with pride. He introduces himself to the group, only with a handshake though. I'm so confused on what the standard way of greeting someone is. I don't want to harass people by giving them three fat French smooches if that's not what they do here.

"Namaste, bitches!" Aagje shouts out. Everyone turns towards her in confusion. Oh lord, she's making a reel for her followers. "Look at this luscious Croatian food, it's giving eco-luxury!" This is the first time I caught Dimi laughing. It's not as thunderously low in pitch as I had expected. He locks eyes with me and we share a cute little "aw, bless her" moment. Whilst Aagje continues her thing, Xen awkwardly shuffles back to make sure they're not in frame. A bit odd, that. I would've thought they'd love to be in Aagje's socials, 'cause she's promoting the retreat after all. Perhaps they're as camera shy as I am.

"I'm here with my girl Elo, she's repping for our neighbours over in France. Say hi girl!" Oh, you've *got* to be shitting me.

"Hi girl." I reply in a semi-whisper. I'm sure I look like a deer caught in headlights. Guess nobody will be following me online anytime soon.

Aagje pats me on the back and continues: "She's a bit more on the introvert side. And over here we have Dimi who comes -"

"Oh, hell no!" He scoots off towards the long dining table. Not even muscle-boy wants to be in the video? How am I - of all people- the only one who ended up in her reel?

Once social media o'clock is over, Josip straightens his back and starts talking about the food. "What we have here today is a mix of traditional Croatian dishes."

"It's all vegetarian though?" Nils wonders.

"It is, yes."

"Aren't Croatians mad about meat?"

"Well - yes." Josip stutters. Nils has this innate talent of making everyone around him feel awkward, it seems. "But we do eat vegetables too, of course."

"Yeah, yeah, I didn't mean you hate vegetables." Once again he looks at my 'can it, boy' frown and zips it. Well done, brother.

"Anyhow. Over here we have Zeljanica."

"Spinach pie?" Esma asks.

"Yes, indeed. How did you know?"

"I'm Bosnian." They exchange smiles.

"Ah, then you'll understand all of this. Very good! Next to that, we have Krompiracha - or?" He gestures at Esma to translate.

"Potato pie."

"Exactly! There's also Sirnica."

"Oh, oh! I know that one!" Dimi chimes in like an eager school boy. This dude definitely has more sides to him than I expected at first. "That's cheese pie!"

## CHAPTER 6

"Oh, another Bosnian in the group?" Josip asks.

"No, I'm Bulgarian. But - you know - Slavic languages and all that."

"Ah yes, my man, we all share similar roots." Josip shifts his attention to the food once more. "So, this one is vegetarian, the first two are vegan. The dough is gluten-free as well, to make sure everyone can try different things."

"Oh, that's glorious!" Aagje adds. "Thanks so much for that, Josip!"

"My pleasure." He looks down a bit coyly. Aagje is definitely in demand in these neck of the woods.

"No Burek?" Milo jokes.

"No meat this week, Milo." Xen replies. "You can survive without it for some days."

"I go home, I eat meat tonight." A loud cackle followed by a slap on his lap. I had heard about Croatians being big on their meat. The poor old man is being deprived of his bare necessities here.

Josip gives Milo a frustrated stare. "Other than the pies, we have roasted vegetable dishes over here and -"

"Locally sourced?" Aagje interrupts.

"Yes, all of it."

A look of absolute relief washes over her face. "Oh, I love that for us. My followers will appreciate it too."

Josip's open mouth signals an "I don't know how to respond to that."

"Sorry, I interrupted you, Josip. I do that when I get excited."

"Meaning, always?" Dimi is getting sassy. I'm here for it.

"Oh! I'm shocked and appalled." She mockingly retorts.

"Anyway." Back to the greens. "On the right side of the table you will find the sesame-based sauces. There's also some smoked Tofu and smoked cheese. For drinks we have basil and elderflower lemonade. Or, there's always water too, of course. It comes from a special local spring said to have healing properties." Of course it does.

"Wait, so no alcohol?" Dimi is back to serious mode.

"No, I'm afraid this week is all about detoxing in all ways possible." Xen shrugs their shoulders apologetically.

Fear has struck his eyes. "Guess I didn't read the fine print. What about ciggies?"

"Cigarettes? We don't encourage it, but I mean - If you've brought some I can hardly forbid you, can I?" Xen is giving off 'I'm not mad, just disappointed' vibes.

"I'm a fag with a fag, you're not taking that away from me." Dimi chuckles. I did *not* expect that sentence from him.

Nils' head shoots upright; that definitely caught his attention. Everyone noticed.

"What?" Dimi reacts.

"Nothing, nothing. I just thought we couldn't say that word if -"

"But, I am. I'm gay. So I'll say what I want about myself."

"You do you, sir." Nils replies. Oh, I sense some kind of tension between those two. The sexual kind, obviously. "Talking about cigarettes, what about grass?"

"What about it, Nils?"

"Is there any available on the premises, or?"

"If you are seriously asking me if I brought weed to my own retreat, the answer is no. But -" Xen throws a mischievous smile his way. "You do you, sir."

"Right, can we eat, people? I'm getting hangry and trust me when I say you do *not* want to mess with hangry Esma."

## CHAPTER 6

The conversation dies down a bit once we all stuff our stomachs with the delicious, luscious, organic, locally sourced, ethically responsible - what did I miss? - food. It's only once our bellies are full that Nils gets the conversation going again.

"So: Xen, Josip, and Milo. You three are the locals here. What can you tell us about Croatians?"

Josip eagerly replies: "Do you mean, what kind of people we are?"

"Yes, exactly. I know there are stereotypes and what-not, but generally speaking: what makes you a Croatian?"

"Franck Jubilarna Kava." Josip replies.

"Come again?"

"It's this type of coffee that we bring to someone's home when we are invited somewhere."

Xen joins in. "I'd add we're good hosts too. We always make sure our guests have plenty of homemade food like dried meat and honey. If we have some local olive oil, we'll usually give it to our guests as well. And of course there's the drinks. You haven't experienced the flavours of Croatia if you haven't tried Rakija. We're quite warm people, Mediterranean in that sense."

"Pomalo." Milo chuckles.

"What does that mean?" Nils asks.

Xen smiles: "It's like this attitude Croatians have, mostly the ones who live by the coast. It means something along the lines of being relaxed, taking things slow."

"I like that." Nils adds. "Pomalo. We need a bit of that in Sweden."

Milo's posture suddenly changes. "Also, being Croatian means surviving the War Of Independence." Milo shifts to a somber tone. That conversation went from chit-chat to deep stuff real quick. The other two Croatians nod their heads in silence.

"Is that the Balkan War from the 90s?"

"No." A harshness that shows us that we need to pay attention to what comes next. "We do not say that. For us, the war is War Of Independence."

The rest of us all look around nervously, not really sure on how to continue the conversation.

"Could I ask -" I start hesitatingly. "Should we avoid this topic? Because I can imagine - well, no I can't, but I'm trying to - that it's still too fresh."

"War killed many. Also on this mountain." I suppose Milo has no problem talking about it then. The other two remain silent though. Either it's to show respect to their older colleague, or it's too personal a topic to breach on the first night. "You see all houses with no people? People run from war to here, up the mountain."

"Did - did you fight during the war?"

"Of course. We all fight."

Esma lowers her head. "My family did too. They were living in Croatia, it was part of Yugoslavia back then, before the war. But they had to flee because of ethnic reasons."

"Ethnic, religious." Milo continues. "It was very bad time. Very, very bad time."

A solemn silence hangs in the air.

Xen breaks it. "Perhaps we can change topics, if that's okay for everyone. The fact of the matter is that we've all lost people in this region. We all have stories, intergenerational traumas, and what-not- but I suggest we leave that for another day."

"I agree. We are not here to focus on the war." Josip says. "We're here to focus on *your* well-being."

"Exactly, Josip, which is why I believe this would be a good

## CHAPTER 6

moment to hold our first Circle of Truth ceremony. We will go around the table and speak truthfully about the reason you have all come here. I will not force anyone to speak, I want you all to feel safe and comfortable, but the floor is yours for those who want to take this moment."

I'm not going first, that's for sure.

"Elo, would you like to start?"

For fuck's sake.

## Chapter 7

Esma's auburn hair absorbs the evening rays just perfectly. It's golden hour and the entire scene looks like it came straight out of a brochure. The light is hitting the dark brown branches of the trees around us, some tender rays frame the people around me beautifully.

I am grateful she decided she wanted to go first after seeing my hesitance.

"At the risk of oversharing on the first night, I told myself I'd be bold." She takes a moment and peers at the sea in the distance, the light breeze caressing her flawless cheekbones. "I'm here, because it's the first time in life I'm allowed to. I don't want to go into too many details concerning the War Of Independence, but all I can safely say is that it screwed my parents up. Financially, mentally - the whole lot. Basically, they decided they didn't want to live in 'normal' society in Bosnia once they were relocated. They had seen and lived through enough for them to want to start anew. So, I ended up being born and growing up in what I thought for the longest time was a commune. It wasn't. Nowhere near it. It was a cult." She turns away from us again and puts her hand on her heart. "I left the cult last year. My brother and parents are still in it. I don't think they realise what they're part of. I sure didn't.

CHAPTER 7

The thing is, once you leave - you *leave*. There's no coming back, no contact to be had, nothing. I haven't seen my family in a year." Teardrops follow their way down to her cheeks, but she doesn't even bother wiping them off. Her eyes aren't here anymore. She's somewhere else. "It was the hardest and most dangerous decision I have taken in my life, but I had to. I was programmed to think and act a certain way for my entire life, so everything in the outside world feels so foreign to me. I don't have a home anymore and a part of me hoped I could find it here, in a healthy version of the world I grew up in. You know, finding spirituality in a way that is *not* toxic. I want to experience what a loving environment means. I love them, you know? My family." She starts sobbing. "And a large part of me feels so guilty about abandoning them. But what kind of parent would allow their kids to be -?" Morbid curiosity takes over, a part of me wants to know what she's been through, but there's no way I would ask. It's up to her to say as much or as little as she wants. I notice Aagje has also started crying. Dimi has put his hand on Esma's shoulder. "Anyway." She shakes off her emotions. "That's why I'm here. I need a safe place free from judgment where I can take my first steps into the outside world."

We all sit in silence for a while, observing the sun set on the mountain top. The moment the sun disappears behind the summit, Xen stands up and switches on the outside lights. It honestly looks gorgeous, these strings of sepia-tinted lights slowly dancing in the evening sky above our heads.

"That was beautiful, Esma. Thanks so much for sharing. If at any moment in time you'd like a one-on-one talk with me or share more with the group, speak up - we're all here for each other." A little crack appears in Xen's voice. They're trying to keep it together, I think. "So, who would like to go next? Keep in mind we don't all *have* to speak tonight, it's completely up to you."

How could I even go after a story like that? My stuff isn't nearly as bad. How could I feel bad for myself when there are other people out there that have gone through so much worse than me?

"I'll go." Dimi replies. I'm a bit surprised, I didn't think he'd speak tonight, but then again the guy is full of mysteries to me.

"Very well, Dimitar."

"Where do I start? Let's see." He lowers his head and glares at the palms of his hands, as if the answers are there. "You all know my name by now, I'm Dimitar. I'm forty-three years old -"

"Oh, really? You look a lot younger, man." Nils adds. Get those two a room already.

"Thanks, it's the skin care routine." He winks at Nils. "Anyway, I'm here because I needed to allow - how can I put this - kindness into my life. I've been in the army for over twenty years." That explains the physique alright. "The only emotions that were allowed were anger. Hard emotions, alpha ones as young people would say. I saw people around me die, year after year. I'm not saying none of us ever cried, but it was mostly done behind closed doors - never in public. It's only when I started meditating that I found some space in my own body. Fuck, I'm not good at wording this in English, sorry."

"Darling, your English is just fine. None of us are natives here, don't you worry." Xen consoles.

"Okay, you make a good point. Still, I get nervous talking in English. What I meant with the space in my body is that it was as if I had this massive block stuck in my chest, like it was all gelled and stuck to the bones, to my rib cage, you know? By focusing on my breath, I visualised making space in my own body. My ribs felt wider. Am I making any sense?"

"You are, Dimitar. Stress and anxiety can often feel like it swallows up your body, in different ways. Coming back to the breathing allows us to make mental space, which often feels like a physical clearing."

*Always come back to the breathing.* Vera used to say that a lot.

"There, exactly, that's what I meant. It became a tool to manage the anxiety. I was finally making some progress, but it all crumbled down when I lost my husband." Oh, shit. "He was sent to a different post. I hadn't seen him in months. The first news I got after two months of silence was that he was shot. Instantly dead. I never got to say goodbye to him." I don't know how he's keeping his composure, I'd be in bits. The straight back might be a facade though, a way for him to mask his emotions. "He died two months ago." Only? And he's here, with a bunch of strangers around him? I mean, *respect.* "That's the short version. The facts. I might get to the rest later, on another day. Thank you for listening, everybody, I appreciate you."

"Could I ask something, please?" Aagje is crying again.

"Of course, Aagje. This is an open circle."

"Would it be rude for me to ask to keep it at that for tonight? I think Esma and Dimi are incredibly brave for being so open, but it's also a lot to take in. If you all want to continue, I completely get it, but then I think I'll leave the circle for now. I don't want to sound selfish or self-absorbed, but it's also important to safeguard my own limits."

"That's a very valid point, Aagje. Let's ask the group, would you all like to call it a night and meet up tomorrow at eight for breakfast?" Not entirely to my surprise everyone agrees straight away. Six of those stories in one evening, after a full day of travelling and settling in, would be way too much. After going around the group hugging and kissing everyone (one kiss each, yep), I head for my tent.

I wish they'd have some of those fairy lights set up here as well, it's completely dark. The soft path underneath my trainers crunches and cracks, but I'm not quite sure where I am. Time to switch on the torchlight on my phone. A subtle hint of unease flows into my body. I've been surrounded by sounds and people all day, going back to solitude and darkness is far scarier than it was in Paris. The phone almost slips from my sweaty hand. I pick up the pace and walk a bit faster. Tomorrow I might ask someone to walk me to my tent, 'cause this is starting to test my nerves. My ears are working overtime, striving to decipher any possibly dangerous sound. But apart from the slight rustling of leaves and the faint voices of the others behind me, all is still.

There it is, finally. My so-called Glamp Tent.

I rush into the tent, switch the night light on and grab my beauty case so I can have a shower before bed. Take a moment, exhale. *You're fine.* I lower my shoulders and exhale through my belly. I hadn't realised how much I've been holding it in, so I released a little gas. *Oh girl,* leave the tent open for a bit. I need to freshen up. A quick shower will work wonders, I'm sure. I just need to grab my towel on the other side of the tent and then I can -

Then I see it.

The silhouette of a man.

Standing there.

Not moving an inch.

## Chapter 8

I clutch onto my towel and study the figure standing outside my tent. I can't move, I'm completely locked in my own body. The man doesn't move either. The wide stance and balled fists terrify me. The tall shadow looks ready to fight.

*Do something.* I can't just sit here, waiting to get attacked. My Swiss pocket knife, how could I forget? I open my suitcase as silently as I can, as if that'll make a difference. He *knows* I'm in here. My hands are trembling, the zipper is jammed. *Come on, not now. Work with me.* I yank it a little harder until it opens.

He's still there. Waiting.

I rummage through my suitcase in the hopes of finding the pocket knife. *Keep it together.* Why can't I stop shaking? There it is. I glance back up.

He's gone. Just like that. I scan the tent from left to right, searching for a shadow or some sort of noise, but nothing. I'm light-headed, so I consciously breathe out - guess I've been holding my breath the entire time. How did he move that fast, and without making a sound? Should I stay put for a bit longer to be sure?

Fuck it, I'm out of here.

I sprint out of the tent, pocket knife in hand, examining the darkness around me. The rustling leaves unnerve me this time around. It's as if they're warning me. I'm not alone. I'm sure of it. I'm at the point of yelling for help when I spot two tall figures moving behind the sturdy tree next to my tent.

There's *two* of them.

Then I hear muffled voices. Hold on, I recognise them. It's Milo and Josip. Was it one of them that was hovering around my tent? A part of me feels relieved that I can place the voices and shadows, but something still feels off. It's the tone of their voices. They're having an argument. Josip's voice is getting louder, but Milo keeps shushing him. My eyes are adjusting to the darkness, and I can almost make out the frustration on both of their faces. I attempt to understand some words, but Croatian is lost on me. Josip keeps repeating one word though: "Horvat." No idea what that means, but it definitely holds an importance in their discussion. *Remember that word.*

Milo throws his hands up in the air, as if showing surrender, and dashes off further down the premises. I should probably go back inside my tent. Hopefully the silhouette I saw earlier was one of the men waiting for the other to arrive. That's probably why I saw the balled fists, whoever it was felt nervous or tense about the conversation they were about to have. Surely that must've been it.

Perhaps my shower can wait till tomorrow morning, when daylight hits.

## Chapter 9

This morning was rough, I won't lie. I woke up feeling groggy from the outside heat and went straight for my shower. It was needed. The cold water soothed my skin and I tried to drown out the fight between Milo and Josip. Being on this 'mission for justice,' of course my entire nervous system is going to stay alert up to the point where I start imagining things. People have arguments, it's no big deal.

I take a look at today's programme on my phone:
08.00 Breakfast
08.30 Circle Meditation
10.00 Mindful Walking
11.30 Solo Meditation
12.00 Lunch
12.30 Kundalini Yoga
14.00 Kimchi Workshop
16.00 Solo Meditation
17.00 EFT Tapping
18.00 Dinner
19.00 Ecstatic Dancing
20.00 Circle of Truth

The schedule looks quite packed, but then again I'm a woman

who loves structure. Give me a day off and I start hyperventilating, not sure what to do with myself or my (at times intrusive) thoughts. Structure and planning keeps me going, it gives me purpose. This schedule might be a bit much though, I didn't exactly wake up fresh.

Breakfast was rather calm, it was mostly spent talking about different types of meditations and their origins. Xen was the only talkative one really, the rest of us listened and took in all the info. Looking around me, I was glad to see the others aren't the chattiest in the morning either. Esma's unkempt hair was quite the contrast to her beautifully coiffed 'do yesterday. She definitely didn't sleep much either. Something else that struck me was Josip's absence. I thought he'd be here to talk about the undoubtedly locally sourced cereals and fruits, but no trace of him. Milo wasn't at the breakfast table either. Apparently Milo is supposed to come back tomorrow, he was off to run errands for his family. An old man like him? Then again, he does look surprisingly lean and healthy for his age. Must be that mountain air. Xen acted weirdly about the whole thing. I tried to push away yesterday night several times, but even during our first meditation round and the forest walk after, the image of that silhouette kept popping into my brain. What if it *wasn't* Milo or Josip? And even if it were, what were they fighting about?

We're about to head for lunch, and I can already tell the solo meditations are going to be the trickiest part of the day. Overanalyzing-me is not ready yet for unguided meditations. Xen has a way of bringing me back whenever I go astray, they have the smoothest - and damn, sexiest - meditation voice, it

## CHAPTER 9

makes me feel supported. I'm not my own strongest support system though, not yet at least. I try to smell the turquoise waters which are kilometres away from me. I imagine the salty air and the endlessness of the waves. I'm sat by one of the best viewing points from the top of the mountain. At least I was lucky enough to spot this place first. I let my nails scratch through the cold earth whilst enjoying all these different hues of green and orange on the mountain and the surrounding forest. The abandoned houses at the foothill jar with the otherwise peaceful vistas. There's something striking about history being so visible in the landscape that it makes me wonder how locals feel about it.

The meditation bell set up at the outside dining table chimes. It's time for lunch. Thank fuck I can be around people again. Now *there's* something I wouldn't have imagined myself thinking after one day.

On my way to lunch I bump into Dimi, he's looking a bit lost in thought.

"Hey Dimi, have you enjoyed the morning so far?"

"Oh - hey Elo! Sorry, I was still half in meditation mode I think."

"No worries. If you want, we can be quiet."

"No, please - The silence was killing me."

"Struggling with the solo part too?"

"You have no idea."

"Who would've thought, the two most introverted people here not enjoying the alone time."

He chuckles. "And the oldest."

"Thanks for the reminder, man." I poke him. "How old are the others again?"

"If I remember correctly, Aagje is twenty-six –"

"For real? She comes across as younger."

"Namaste, bitches!" Dimitar shouts out. We both burst out in laughter.

"Yeah, that might be why. Anyway, how about the others?"

"Esma told me she was nineteen."

"Ah, the Benjamin of the group then."

"The what-now?"

"In French we call the youngest of a group the Benjamin."

"Why?"

"Eh, good question. No idea really. Ha. How old is Nils?"

"Twenty-three."

"You didn't have to think long about that one, did you?" I wink at him.

"What is that supposed to mean?"

"Oh come on, don't play dumb with me. I've seen the way you two interact. He's got a thing for you and if you ask me, it's reciprocated."

A gentle smile forms on Dimi's face. "Could be. But he's so young!"

"Hey, no judgment here, I get it! Those eyes."

"The dreads though, they're something else."

"You're telling *me*? He called me *sis*."

"No, for real? I would've thought their generation was more politically correct."

"Me too, but maybe that's more of an American thing."

"By the way, talking about crushes: what about you and Xen?"

Damn, I thought I was being subtle, but then again saying "hello, I'm a lesbian" probably isn't that smooth of an introduction. "Xen? I mean, they're gorgeous, don't get me wrong,

## CHAPTER 9

but they're our teacher."

"Doesn't that make it even hotter? A little teacher - student thing."

"Gross! No, I admit I'm attracted, but I won't act on it." They probably wouldn't be interested in me anyway, I'm a basket case.

"Tell yourself whatever you want, *sis*. Something tells me there might be some blossoming summer romances in the making."

"Some? So you *are* including you and Nils?"

"How perceptive. It's funny how we're so focused on the meditation and the courses, but the moment we're off, it's like we all revert back to high school talk."

"Ha, you're right. I guess it makes the coursework a little lighter. Don't get me wrong, I'm enjoying most of what we've done so far, but it also gets a little heavy."

"Exactly, so why not have a little fling?"

There's a tiny part of me that wants to ask "Didn't your husband die just two months ago?" but that'd be so rude. Everyone copes with grief in different ways. He probably needs the lightness, the distraction.

When we arrive at the dining table, Nils is smiling from ear to ear at Dimi and showing him he saved a seat. How adorable, that little non-PC brother of mine. Aagje is the first to speak to me. "Hey Elo, want to sit next to me?" Her hair is done up in two long braids, making her look even younger.

"Sure, thanks!" I take a seat next to Aagje and nod at Esma and Xen who are seated across from me.

"Today's lunch is a mix of Indian and South Korean fusion mezzes." I turn around and notice Josip has turned up for lunch. He glances at me and then looks away again quickly. He's got a black eye. Milo has got some punch left in him, apparently.

"What is up with his eye?" Aagje whispers at me. I'm not sure I should tell her - or anyone for that matter - about yesterday evening.

"No idea. Looks like he got into a fight."

"Not very spiritual, is it?" She giggles. "He needs to open up his heart Chakra if you ask me."

Maybe I can tell the others tonight about the fight once Xen and Josip are off to bed. Xen claps their hands together loudly, startling almost everyone at the table. "Right! I wanted to thank you all for being so open and cooperative this morning. How has it been so far?"

Esma is the first to reply again. "Fun! Okay, maybe fun is not the right way to put it, but I'm truly enjoying myself. It's the first time I get to experience these meditation sessions with other people. It's odd, really, how we've all only just met each other yesterday and I already feel so at ease with everyone."

"That's delightful to hear, Esma, thank you for being so open."

"I agree." Nils adds. "I especially liked the mindful walk in the forest and around the mountain top. There was something so peaceful about being around like-minded people without having to talk. I loved hearing the cicadas, the crunchy leaves on the path, all of that nature and us. It may sound weird, but I felt proud at the time."

Xen tilts their head. "Proud? How so, Nils?"

"Just the fact that I took the risk to come out here to Croatia on my own, without knowing anyone else. Also, opening up to other people. You might've heard the stereotype about Swedes not being the warmest people. Sadly, I agree with that. I'm trying to fight against that cliche though. So yeah, walking around with you all and being part of something bigger than merely my own interest made me proud. Of myself, but also of everyone here."

That's quite sweet of him, to be fair. Whenever people open up like that, my initial response is 'yuck, that's cringe' or 'cheesy', but there's something refreshing about being surrounded by people who are unapologetically real. The cringe part is probably because of the way I was raised back in Curacao. It was never safe to express my emotions without them being mocked by my parents. So anyone who would be emotional, I'd regard as weak. In retrospect, I suppose *I* was the weak one.

"Beautiful. Well, my gorgeous people, time to eat up! We have a full afternoon ahead of us."

# Chapter 10

The afternoon went by rather quickly, quite possibly because the schedule was so packed. The yoga and EFT tapping workshops were really enjoyable, even though the EFT one made me cry. Well, I should add that it made *everyone* in the group cry. I had heard about that tapping technique releasing traumas, but I wasn't too sure it would work. Well, fuck me it did. We were all a sobbing mess by the end of it. Nobody explained why they were crying and frankly, I was quite happy about that. I couldn't do the 'Kumbaya circle' thing all day. It's good to work through some things on my own too without having to talk about it. The others don't need to know about my hospital bills or my past in Curacao.

   The Kimchi workshop was hilarious. For me, anyway. I know I'm not the best cook, but I thought I could at least pickle some vegetables and put them in a fermentation jar. Turns out there are a whole lot more steps to it and in my case, breaking two jars was part of the experience too. Xen was so patient with me though, they hung around me most of the time when I was messing up again. I noticed Dimi's approving stares. It's not like he's any better. Nils and him are always seated next to each other, even though Nils hasn't mentioned being gay or queer or anything. It could just be a budding friendship. Or perhaps

CHAPTER 10

Nils is Ace, I shouldn't assume everyone needs sex just because I do.

Once I found my little mountaintop safe-haven, I did my best to be kind to myself during the second solo meditation of the day. I was able to clear most of my head this time around, up to the point where I even turned off all future worries and anxieties about the past. Perhaps it only lasted for a few seconds, but it was a victory for me.

Then *he* showed up. That awful mask. The only thing in my vision: the white Buddha mask, surrounded by smokey black clouds. It set off the beginning of a panic attack, but I managed to open my eyes, stand up, and do some jumping jacks. They usually get me out of fight or flight, or at its worst even freeze. Fuck that mask. Tomorrow I'll start looking for clues around the house. There must be *something*. Milo and Josip could be hiding evidence. Xen, too, don't forget about them. Don't fall for someone who might play a role in Vera's death. I have to remind myself now and then, because it is easy to get carried away on this retreat.

After another lovely dinner - including a grumpy Josip and still no sign of Milo -, we walked up the first floor of the house past the sound bowl healing room - to a little dance room I don't think Xen showed us last night. Little, but with high ceilings and big windows. The first thing Xen did after entering the room was turn off the lights.

Time for ecstatic dancing. I think I have officially annihilated my comfort zone. You should've seen me, honestly. The session started with rather slow, flowy instrumental music. We were all supposed to close our eyes the entire time and dance in whatever way felt right. At first, I felt too self-conscious to move at all. I thought "well, if they have their eyes closed anyway I might as well not move at all, they won't know" until Aagje crashed into me. In a way, I'm glad I opened my eyes in the beginning to see that everyone looked equally unbalanced and freaky. This is some white-people shit.

"Just go with it." Aagje whispered and continued her rag-doll-esque moves. So I did, hesitant at first, a little stiff after, until I got to a point where I genuinely couldn't give a rat's arse if I looked ridiculous - 'cause we *all* did.

The tempo of the music went up a bit, number by number. I lost track of time, but by the end of it, I was soaking in sweat. It was cool to open our eyes and see everyone looking tired, out of breath, and the happiest we'd been all day.

# Chapter 11

We are all seated around the campfire at the back of the house. Xen, Dimi, Aagje, Esma, Nils, and me. It brings me back to my twenties and being surrounded by friends at the beach. Thinking about it now, I'm not sure they were ever my friends. None of them reached out when I told them I had to move to Paris. The silence became deafening. This might be the first time in my life that I am surrounded by people who accept me for me. It is giving peace, Aagje would say.

"Thanks for today, Xen. The dancing was awesome!" Nils says enthusiastically.

"My pleasure, love! Glad to hear."

"It's mad. One day here feels like a week elsewhere." He adds.

"I agree. This is the most I have gotten out of a day since –" Since before cancer hit my world. I can't say it. "Since a long time."

"It's so endearing seeing you all open up so early on. I *knew* we selected the right people. On that note, are we okay with doing a second round of Circle of Truth?"

I'm not sure. Today has been a lot. I look around the circle to see how the others feel. Nils is still full of energy. "I'll go!" He takes a beat. "Unless anyone else wants to, of course." The rest of the group appears more than happy to let him have his moment. I'm warming up to him. He's young and he's blunt, but there's a lot of kindness there too.

"Okay, here goes nothing." His body language shifts into a bag of nerves. The poor guy, I didn't expect that. "I spent my entire youth in foster care." Bombshell. In my head, this dude has had everything given to him on a silver platter. "My birth mom was an alcoholic and I don't even know who my real dad is, so I ended up in foster care. I stayed with five different families over the course of sixteen, maybe seventeen years. It never worked out. I was always too much, too demanding, too rebellious, too - ADHD." How do these people even do it: sum up their entire lives filled with misery in just a couple of sentences? It's like they've practiced for an elevator pitch or something. I wouldn't know where to start or what to omit. Nils takes a slow inhale and continues: "I'm not saying any of this to get a pity party out of you people. If I'm being real, I kind of just want to get it out in the open, so you know something about me and we can all move on. Anyway, my birth mom died when I was eighteen. I found out through one of my foster parents who had decided they wanted to tell me about her if I agreed, which I did. She had overdosed. Miraculously, I ended up with an inheritance - a big one at that. My mom was not poor, in fact, she was part of the Swedish aristocracy and I was conceived out of wedlock, so I was given a large sum to basically shut up and pretend I never existed. That's how I have felt for most of my life anyway. As if I don't actually exist. Unworthy." He's damn courageous for keeping it real like that. "So I put on a brave face, a loud mouth, and a big grin. That way nobody could ever truly get to know me." Aagje is crying, that girl is definitely the sensitive one of the group. However, to my surprise so is

## CHAPTER 11

Dimi. Nils lets out one unexpectedly loud sob, takes a pause, and then finishes his story. "I was too young to have that much money. I partied too hard with the wrong people and ended up in rehab by the age of twenty." Christ almighty, this fella is twenty-three and he has lived more lives than the rest of us combined. "I've been sober since then and I have set up a charity for foster kids. Even then, after helping so many kids, my core stayed invisible. Spirituality and mindfulness are what finally started bringing me back to myself. That's why I am here. Because I don't want to feel unworthy anymore."

"Thank you for your honesty, Nils." Xen takes his hand and puts it between theirs. "We see you here." Dimi stands up out of nowhere and goes in to hug Nils. They both cry in silence.

Aagje shuffles closer to me and whispers: "I can't go after that. I'm just an influencer who got a sponsorship deal." Her eyes are full of terror. "They'll hate me for not having had a rough life."

"No, they won't, silly. But nobody is forced to speak." I whisper back. "I don't feel like it either tonight. Maybe tomorrow."

"Anyone else?" Xen scans the group, but we all remain silent. "That is absolutely fine. I believe it is best for me to hit the hay, so I can let you have a little chat amongst yourselves." It's not even eleven in the evening, but it does feel later after such a busy day. "So, good night lovelies and see you bright and early for breakfast!" I still want to get to know Xen better, but I tell myself tomorrow morning at breakfast is the moment. No more stalling. If they have any connections to Vera or what happened, I can't keep procrastinating. It's odd. I came here with a purpose, but the moment I met these people, it was as if my 'mission' was pushed to the back of my mind.

"Sorry if that was a bit too intense." Nils mutters to us once Xen has left.

"Not at all, it was courageous if anything," Dimi replies and gives him another hug. They're so cute together. Whatever is happening between them, I'm happy to see it.

"Guys, did you notice Josip's eye today?" Aagje asks out of nowhere.

"It was kind of difficult to miss," Dimi replies. "What do you think happened to him?"

"I bet it was a bar fight!" Nils chimes in. "He's probably the kind of guy who -"

"Hey! That's a bit rude, Nils." Esma protests. "We're not supposed to be judgmental, remember? Perhaps something serious has happened to him."

Oh damn, I can't keep it to myself anymore. Fuck it. "I heard him get into a serious discussion with Milo yesterday evening by my tent." I spit out.

"Aca-scuse me?" Aagje looks offended. "Why didn't you tell me?"

I'm flattered, I didn't know we were - at least according to her - that close yet. "I didn't know how to. Xen was always around. I figured it was best to wait until they're gone."

"Oh, I see." That calmed her right down. Collision avoided. "Juicy though!"

"Spill the tea!" Dimi shouts out. Everyone turns their heads at him. "What? I'm not *that* old. I know what young people say." Aagje, Esma, and Nils crack up.

"I don't know what to spill, frankly. I don't speak Croatian. All I know is one of them was hovering by my tent at first."

"What? That's creepy!" Esma takes my hand. All this hand-grabbing, it's turning into The Drew Barrymore Show over

## CHAPTER 11

here.

"I know! Anyhow, once I left my tent to check it out, I saw them. They were practically shouting at each other. By the way, Esma, there *was* one word Josip kept repeating."

"Oh, really? What was it? I can probably understand it, Bosnian is very close to Croatian."

"All he kept saying was "Horvat" this, "Horvat" that. What does that mean?"

Esma's mouth opens wide. "It's - It's a surname."

"Then why do you look so terrified?"

"Because of Ivan Horvat."

"Who?" Dimi asks.

"Wait, none of you have heard of Ivan Horvat?"

Nobody has.

Esma puts on an evil smirk. "Buckle up kids, because you're in for one *heck* of an urban legend."

## Chapter 12

"You're seriously going to tell us a horror story over a campfire?" Dimi asks a bit haughtily.

"If you don't want to hear it, I won't tell it obviously."

"No, no, ignore him! No offense, Dimi!" Nils shrugs his shoulders at him.

"None taken, I guess."

"Okay then, you better not interrupt me! So, Ivan Horvat is known all around Trnovac. It was my cousin who first told me the story. I've never forgotten about it since. People around here say there used to be a young boy named Ivan who was raised extremely spiritually, like Buddhism on crack, by his parents in the 90s. They were both intellectuals and worked for a local charity shop studying Eastern spiritual philosophy. You know, the locals thought they were a bit different. Spirituality wasn't that common yet at that time, definitely not when the tensions in the region started rising. Anyhow, any time Ivan would come home and he'd be late, or his shoes would be too dirty from playing around in the mountain, they'd punish him. Trust me, you don't want to hear the uncensored version of the story. Let's just say they were *nasty* to him."

"Wait, but how is that Buddhist? Punishment doesn't sound very kind." Aagje remarks.

## CHAPTER 12

"That's why I said 'on crack'. They believed in some very niche form of spirituality. Some even say Ivan's parents were practicing black magic."

"Black magic isn't the same as spirituality though. It's not like we're evil witches or wizards." Nils protests.

"I know, obviously. But to some people, black magic is the opposite of spirituality, or the extreme version of it. If you ask me, the townspeople were probably scared of them, because they believed in something that most didn't at the time. Back to Ivan. Teachers started noticing his behaviour becoming more and more erratic, he started getting rage fits and he would also turn more and more inward and stop talking to the small number of friends he had left. The parents didn't want to talk to any of the teachers. When the war started, Ivan barely came to school. Nobody knows whether he had to stay at home or whether he was out there up the mountain on his own. At the end of the school year, he had failed the year. The neighbours heard the family having a massive fight that evening and one woman said she saw the parents literally throwing Ivan out of the house. The parents were scholars, so this kind of failure reflected poorly on them. That was it. He was only seven. They were so ashamed of their son failing that he wasn't welcome anymore. Shortly after, Ivan's parents moved to Montenegro. The years after several villagers spotted him around the area. Whenever they tried talking to him, he walked off and didn't reply. Nobody has heard him utter a word since he was kicked out. As the years went by and the war ended, people rarely saw him. When they did, he was either staying in one of the many abandoned houses or they'd find him sitting alone in nature, eyes closed, in some meditative state. Around that time, much of the livestock started disappearing. Many sheep carcasses were found in those empty houses. Then people started disappearing too, always tourists." I was wondering when the story would turn scary. There we have it, yup. "The local police force would find corpses of tourists, half-eaten. They were usually horribly mangled too." Oh, good lord. I put my hair in a bun, 'cause this shit is getting *intense.*

"Wait, wait - so the police *knew* about this Ivan kid and still allowed tourists to come up here?" Dimi asks apprehensively.

"First of all, by that time he was a young adult. And second, the police went on so many searches, but he was always one step ahead. Nobody has seen him since the first human corpse was found about twenty years ago. But each year, there are still some people who end up being lost - and not always found."

"So people think he's still living around here?" I wonder. Vera. The killer. This is the clue I've been waiting for, for three years. I know it's a story, but there might be some truth to it.

"Well, people are still disappearing according to these stories. It never makes it into the local news, but I've read some foreign articles on Reddit. I know how that sounds, trust me, I do."

"Explain this to me, Esma." Aagje sounds more serious than I have ever heard. "If you knew about this potential serial killer roaming the mountain, why the actual fuck would you come here? *Here*, of all places?"

Esma stutters. "I-I have family here and in Split. I told you. The family that didn't move with my parents to Bosnia. I have an uncle and aunt in Split - well, I used to have a niece too, but she moved to Brussels years ago and passed away. However, most of the family should still live in this area of Croatia."

"So, they're not part of the cult?" Nils wonders.

"No, they don't even know about it. I haven't met any of them, except for one cousin in Split who I've been texting with.

## CHAPTER 12

I'm here because I want to find my family, to build up a life again."

"But why wouldn't you contact the rest of your family online or anything?" I ask.

"They're older people, Elo, they probably don't even have internet. I wanted to start here, at the retreat, to build myself up. To find the strength and the courage to go look for them after this week."

"Even if you believe there is a killer hanging around?"

"Nils, listen: I don't know if I believe that story or not. But I know the impact this man has had on my family. My mother couldn't shut up about it. Ivan this, Ivan that. She believed he had stolen the sheep from her farm. Does that mean he is an actual killer? No idea. I'm not here for him, I'm here for my family." Why is she being so defensive? I need to ask this: "Did anyone ever notice something particular about - about the way he was dressed?" Please say he wore a Buddha mask, *please*.

"No, just that he wore old rags obviously that he had outgrown and that he is a tall, strong man who doesn't speak." Damn.

"Basically a Croatian knock-off of Jason Voorhees?" Dimi snickers.

"Who?"

"That masked killer from "Friday the 13th". You know, the guy in the hockey mask."

"Oh, that's his name? Well, I suppose so. That's all I know about the story. People here really believe he exists."

Something hits me. "Our entire group is foreign."

"So?" Nils replies.

"*So*? If this Horvat man only kills people who aren't local, don't you think it's a bit of a coincidence that the only Croatians here are our teacher and two men who were fighting with each other?"

"Do you think they're behind this? Hold on Eloise, you're not actually buying any of this crap, are you?" Of course the white dude doesn't believe the story. Go fucking figure.

"I don't know! Maybe?"

"Elo, it's a *story* - an urban legend. Every little town has one."

"Said every straight white brother ever before they get sliced and diced." I fire back.

"Who said I'm straight?" Oh. Damn, why would I even say that? I feel guilty for a hot second until I see Dimi's eyes light up. You're welcome, fam.

"Okay people, I think it's best we go to bed and talk to Xen about this in the morning. It's been a long day and I don't think getting caught up in some local horror folklore is the best idea at night." Dimi tries to rationalise the situation.

"Go to bed, *now*? *Alone*, after that story? Great." Aagje sighs.

"We'll walk you ladies." Dimi smiles. "Like you said, it's a story. If we need clarification, we can ask the three locals in the morning."

"Yes, 'cause they'll definitely tell us if they're part of the scheme. Clever." I had almost missed my own sarcasm. "Fine, let's get some sleep. I better not die first."

"Don't worry, Elo, it's usually the blondes." Aagje smiles, followed by a barely audible: "Oh, fuck me."

## Chapter 13

After having said goodnight to Esma, Nils, and Aagje, Dimitar and I walk further down the grounds to my tent. He is smoking his cigarette and seems to enjoy it now that he doesn't get the chance to smoke all the time.

I open up my tent and crawl in. I turn back and say: "Thanks Dimi, appreciate it."

He ponders for a few seconds, then replies: "You *do* know it's just a story?"

"You *do* know that it's always the men who don't take shit seriously in horror movies?"

He stands there, his mouth open.

"Well?"

"I guess you're right. Still, we shouldn't get worked up over this."

"Right, I see." There's no point in convincing him tonight, that's obvious.

"Good night, Elo." He ducks down and gives me a quick kiss on the cheek.

Shockingly, I can't sleep tonight. I keep thinking about Esma's story. Ivan Horvat - is there any way he's connected to Vera's death? I mean, she did say he goes for tourists. Buddhism, spiritual retreat, a flipping Siddharta mask: it all adds up, right? It must do, there are too many coincidences. Who else could be in on it though? Xen acted all weird when I asked where Milo and Josip were this morning. And then there's Esma: she knows an awful lot about this Horvat character. Why would she come back to this mountain after hearing those stories? Unless she's also looking for closure. My mind is being thrown back and forth the entire goddamn time and it doesn't matter which meditation technique I try or which healing stones I put on my chest – nothing works. What if it was *him* who stood outside my tent yesterday? Watching, waiting to kill? Oh lord, I'm losing my marbles.

Crunching leaves.

Someone's walking down the path next to me. Approaching my tent.

I inhale sharply.

This time I know where my pocket knife is. I kept it at the ready. My heart races in my throat. The steps are slow, yet confident. I recognise that walk.

The silhouette is growing larger and more ominous. They're still some steps away.

Just a story, *my ass.* I knew I shouldn't listen to those boys.

Bring it on then, Ivan, I'm ready.

I ignore the stinging sensation prodding my scalp and rock back and forth, balancing my core for what's ahead.

The silhouette is now the same size it was yesterday night and standing still in front of my tent. The shadow subtly nudges closer, inching a mere metres from the entrance of my makeshift home.

*Come on then, bastard.*

The shadow of a hand moves towards the zipper of the tent.

## CHAPTER 13

I put the knife in front of me and stretch out my arm.
This is it.

# Chapter 14

The zipper is being opened.

I rush towards the shadow and cry out: "I've got a knife, you fucker!"

A high-pitched scream rolls back at me. "Stop, it's me! Aagje!"

What? What is *she* doing here?

"Elo, let me in, please!"

Something has happened. I can tell the moment she jumps inside the tent and closes the zipper behind her. She's dripping in sweat, it's almost a relief to see her looking less than perfect for once. She's human after all.

"What happened to you?"

"I was going over my angel cards - oh, by the way, Michael's card mentioned something about a flow of healing waters and a big transformation ahead - and all of a sudden there was someone outside my tent, Elo, I swear! You *have* to believe me!"

"I do, I do!" I grab onto her wrists and pull her closer. She needs to know I take her seriously. "What did you see exactly?"

"A silhouette, a shadow of a man - just like you described. Tall, broad shoulders."

"Did you see any weapons on him, or - ?"

## CHAPTER 14

"No, nothing. He was standing still like he was hoping for me to react."

"And then what?"

"Then he walked away, slowly. I waited until the shadow was entirely gone and then I ran straight here."

I try to gather my thoughts for a moment before suggesting: "Let's go to the tents of Dimi and Nils. If they're the ones being pervy, it needs to be stopped. Tonight."

"Dimi and Nils? Why on earth would they -?"

"I'm not sure, but they're the only two men who are close by. We need to be sure we can trust them."

We walk back out, hand in hand, me with the Swiss pocket knife and Aagje with her phone in hand, torchlight on. Somehow having Aagje by my side takes away the fear I had before. Well, perhaps not entirely in all fairness, but I have this sense of urgency that overpowers any other emotions. We pick up the pace and head for Dimi's tent first, as he's the bulkier one of the two.

Aagje shines her torch onto his tent. "Dimi?" She whispers. No answer.

"Dimitar, are you there?" I shout. Aagje glances at me. Whispering obviously doesn't work girl, I don't have time for this. "Dimi!"

"Wh-what?" A sleepy voice replies from inside the tent. "What's up?"

We see the tent open up, and a rough-looking Dimi walking out. "What's going on?"

Aagje and I look at each other. It's not him. It can't be.

"Aagje saw a silhouette of a guy standing in front of her tent."

"What, for real? The same thing that happened to you, Elo?"

"Exactly. We wanted to make sure -"

"That it wasn't me?" He exhales. "I get it. You're only trying to make sure. Have you checked Nils' tent?"

"No, he's next." Aagje responds.

"Wait, I was first?"

"You're the muscle-man, sorry. The dude looked huge." She explains.

Dimi smirks. "I'll take that as a compliment."

"When you're done with your ego tripping, can we check out Nils' tent, please?"

"Sorry Elo, I - absolutely, let's go!"

Aagje, Dimi, and I walk further down the path towards Nils' tent.

"Nils, dude, wake up!" Yeah, Dimi's voice would've come in handy before.

"Dimi? What?" A moment of silence. "Do - do you want to come in?" A flirty voice comes from inside. Dimi turns bright red. "No, I - not now, I meant -"

Oh for fuck's sake, get it together already. I interrupt: "Open your tent, Nils!"

Another droopy-eyed face meets us, looking beyond tired. "Why are you all here?"

"Aagje saw a man outside of her tent, the way Elo did yesterday." Dimi summarises.

"Holy - do you think it was Milo or Josip?"

"I don't know. All I know is that it freaked me out. I'm not going back in there on my own."

"You can sleep next to me, Aagje." I suggest.

"Are you sure?"

"Absolutely."

She drops her shoulders and shows the first signs of relief.

## CHAPTER 14

"Thanks so much!"

Suddenly, another torchlight momentarily blinds all of us. We scream our lungs out.

I hold onto my knife.

"Wait, wait, it's me!" Esma turns off her torchlight and scans our faces questioningly. "What are you all doing outside?"

## Chapter 15

I jolt up, sweat beads sticking to my forehead. Oh lord, my bonnet smells horrible. The mask came back to haunt me in my dreams. Aagje opens her eyes as I grab my phone.

"Elo?"

"Yes? Sorry, did I wake you up?"

"It's fine. What time is it?"

I glance at my screen. "Twenty past seven."

"How on earth is it this hot already? It's giving sauna." We both smile.

I open the zipper and let the morning breeze in. "That's better." These tents are cool for most of the day, but in the early mornings it's like I'm in a hot yoga session.

Aagje is staring into nothingness. Her mind is elsewhere. "Aagje, come back to me. What's up?"

"Oh - I'm - I was thinking about yesterday evening. A part of me was hoping it was all a dream."

"I'm afraid not. How are you feeling now?" I prefer focusing on *her* emotions rather than mine.

"Confused. What if what I saw wasn't actually real?"

"How so?"

"Like, what if I was imagining this silhouette, 'cause I got scared due to that Horvat story?"

## CHAPTER 15

"Aagje, *girl*, it's bad enough the men here rationalise everything - please don't go there. Esma and I believe you, we need to talk to Xen and figure this out together."

"Uhu." She's not convinced. We step outside of the tent, stretching our limbs and taking in the nature and quietude around us. Silence before the storm. Anxiety sits in the pit of my stomach, hoping today I will finally get some answers. Aagje looks sullen, deflated even.

"Aagje?"

"What?"

"I need to tell you something."

"Sure."

"I'm sorry for being snarky when we first met." She doesn't reply, but instead looks straight ahead at the sea waves. "I haven't had the best track record with friendships or any kind of relationships for that matter. I came in here bitter and angry with the world."

"I know." Her tone is calm and collected.

"You do?"

"It was fairly obvious. At least to me. I sense these things, more than most people."

"You do, don't you? Anyway, I'm really sorry if I made you feel any kind of way. You're awesome."

She nods and lowers her head. Somehow her energy is still blue. "It's fine."

"It doesn't look like you're fine. Aagje, you can be real with me. I know I came in prejudiced and bitchy. I'm really sorry."

She lifts her head and turns towards me for the first time during the conversation. "It's not you, Elo. It's people, in general. They take a quick glance at me and they've made up their minds before even getting to know me. It's the fillers and the botox, the social media aspect. Parts of me look fake, so people assume *I* am too."

Damn, I hit a nerve there.

"So I don't blame you per se. Guess it would be nice if people took the time to see who I am. I end up faking it, because that's what people expect."

"Namaste, bitches?" I smile. To my relief, she smiles back.

"Exactly. Sometimes it's easier to go along with the stereotype people have about me."

"Circle of truth? Why *are* you here?" I knew there was more to her story, but then again I definitely judged her as well. Fuck, I should've known better. I'm a grown-ass woman.

Aagje takes a slow breath in and out. "There *is* a promo deal. That's not a lie. However, there's more to it than that."

"Hey, girls!" Esma pops up from behind her tent, heading our way. Crap, bad timing.

Aagje appears jittery all of a sudden. "Anyway, I'll tell you more later. Apology accepted." She squeezes my arm.

Esma comes in for a hug and a kiss, even though I warn her I'm all sticky. She looks the way she did on the first evening during golden hour. She's definitely been up for a while. How people can look glam in the morning is beyond me.

"You slept in Eloise's tent?" She asks Aagje.

"Yeah. How about you?"

"The boys slept next to me, they kept their promise. It was a bit cramped, but at least I felt safe."

"They didn't start fooling around next to you?" I wink at Esma. She cracks up.

"Not as far as I'm aware, but those two - you're right. It's only a matter of time. I think Nils is holding back, because Dimi is so much older."

## CHAPTER 15

"I think it's more so because Dimi has only recently lost his partner." Aagje semi-corrects Esma.

"Well, there's that too, of course. So, what's the game plan for this morning? Are we walking straight up to Xen with a multitude of questions?"

"Is there another way?" I question.

"Probably not. Perhaps we can ease our way into the conversation over breakfast. Like, not go in too strong. We don't want them to close off." Esma makes a good point.

"You're right. Anyway, I'm going to take a quick shower and I'll head over for breakfast."

"I'll join you, Elo, I'm a stinky mess."

"No comment." Esma waves her hand in front of her nose. "The boys are already at the breakfast table, but we'll wait for you two."

## Chapter 16

You can tell there's a nervous energy at the breakfast table. We're all waiting for Xen to arrive, so they can - hopefully - elaborate on the entire Ivan Horvat story. If I word it right, perhaps I can bring in Vera's murder and the Buddha mask too. I've done jack shit so far, coming in all hot and ready to decipher some murder case, when in the end I've been meditating and making friends instead. Perhaps *that's* what I really came here for and Vera was the excuse. I'm not too sure anymore.

Xen approaches the table and gives us a gentle wave. I pull my locks together and get ready for whatever is about to unravel.

"Good morning, lovelies." Their smile is off. Something has happened. Aagje scans my face and nods. She feels it too. "How have you all been? I do want to apologise about breakfast. It's not as lush and well-presented as yesterday, but Josip hasn't shown up this morning."

The five of us all look at each other.

"Was he supposed to?" I ask, not allowing any more time to be wasted.

"Of course, he takes care of all the meals."

"But he wasn't here yesterday morning either."

Xen glares down at their plate. "That - that was planned. Not today though. Anyhow, -" They look back up and touch their

## CHAPTER 16

feather earring. "Nothing I can't handle."

We all dig in and start eating the pots of yoghurt and fresh slices of fruit. How do I even start the conversation? Get Xen to open up first, so they're caught off guard after.

"Xen?"

"Yes, Elo?"

"I was wondering about something the other day." The others all frown. I know people, give me a moment. I'll get there.

"Do go on, lovely." Something about their tone isn't authentic today.

"When I first met you, you said your pronouns were she and they, right?"

"Correct."

"How does that work in Croatian? Are there specific pronouns for non-binary people, like in French and Swedish?"

Esma gives me a little "What does that have to do with yesterday?" expression.

"Oh - right. I didn't expect that question. It's a tough one to answer actually. You see, Croatian is a very gendered language. Everything has a gender, even down to the verb conjugations. So, using "they" like in English wouldn't work. The rest of the sentence would still be signalling either a male or female perspective. There have been many seminars around this topic lately, and one option could be using a specific past tense that is without gender. The problem is that almost nobody uses this verb tense and we'd have to speak about the present or future, using a past tense." Everyone is sucked into the explanation. They're definitely opening up, and - in all honesty - this is quite interesting. "So, that is very unlikely to happen. Another change I've noticed in the queer community is that younger people at times start abandoning Croatian altogether and revert to English, as the pronouns are clearer and the anglophone perspective is more inclusive and forward-thinking."

Right, how do I steer this talk into the Horvat story? "So, would you say Croatia is a bit more attached to tradition?"

"I think generalising is always dangerous. Things have changed a great deal since we've become independent and we're part of the EU now too, as you know." Their body posture is finally more relaxed. It's working. "But perhaps because we are such a young country, a lot of us do want to hold onto certain elements of tradition."

"Like folklore?" Dimi jumps in. Good man.

"Yes, for example. Our traditional music and clothes -"

"And stories?" Nils is a tad bit too enthusiastic, as per usual.

"Stories?"

"Like, Urban Legends and stuff." Oh, careful there Nils. That's really direct.

"Actually, yes." Xen lights up. "We have so many folkloric tales about the region, often a mix of fairy tales and fantasy. Everyone always talks about Norse gods and goddesses, or Greek and Roman ones. There are so many interesting sagas about Slavic gods and goddesses too. Stories about fertility, harvests, and- " And murder?

"How about the Ivan Horvat story?"

We all freeze. Nils has dropped the bomb. Now it's a matter of time to see how Xen will react.

"How - who told you about - about that man?" They are struggling to form a proper sentence.

"I did." Esma replies truthfully. "Like I said earlier, Xen, I have family here. They used to tell my parents about Ivan Horvat, the serial killer."

## CHAPTER 16

"I don't see why we should entertain such tales, really." Xen shakes their head in disgust. "Stories like that are very low on the vibration scale and tend to hold a negative impact on your Root Chakra." Bullshit. Nils and Esma try to reply, but are shut down quickly. "Honestly, why would we talk about a serial killer at a mindfulness retreat? It goes against everything that we stand for here." Xen is getting flustered and for the first time - angry. "Anyway, as I said, Josip hasn't shown up this morning and Milo is only coming back tonight. That means I'll have to change the schedule around a bit. Finish up your breakfast and we'll head straight to the sound healing session." I try to get a little extra question in, but they're rambling on. "After that, you'll all have some solo meditation time, so I can prepare lunch for you in the meantime. We still have food for three days, so we'll be fine, but I'm not that good of a cook compared to Josip." A forced smile appears on their lips. "But I will do my absolute best nonetheless! Right, beautiful people, finish up, and let's head for the sound healing room!"

I want to shout out "But Aagje and I saw silhouettes in front of our tent!", but I'm scared of how Xen would react at this point. The only thing we can do for now is do the sound healing session and come back later for lunch, when Xen is less stressed about the uprooting of the schedule, with more - less direct, no names (Nils) - questions. We've gone in too strong.

"All done? Great, let's head for our first session of the day!"

## Chapter 17

I try not to lose it this time, walking into the sound healing room. It doesn't sit right with me, to start a session when Xen is obviously not at their best and we have so many questions. What else can we do? Disrupt the entire thing?

"Would you mind leaving the doors open, Xen?" Esma asks. "It's a bit hot in here."

"Sure, lovely, I'll crack the window open too." A soft wind envelops us all as we lay down on the cosy rugs. I take another look at the opened window. Vera's window. That's it, I'm not going to stop the questioning at lunch until we get the answers we need.

"Could I ask you all to close your eyes and follow the sounds? Let the sound bowls be your guide into your inner thoughts, and your emotions. Don't block them, but allow them to flow alongside the melodies. Whatever comes up, whether it be positive or what you consider to be negative, all emotions are welcome here. All thoughts are valid and are what they are - thoughts. Do not judge them."

The swirling sounds almost instantly calm me down. I didn't expect that to be possible today, but I'll gladly take it. This is the first moment since yesterday when I am not in some state

## CHAPTER 17

of emergency. I hear the mellow breathing of the people around me, the people I found a new home with. Even if it's temporary. The colours come back up, the way they usually do. The light pink dominates the spectrum, cleansing the anxiety and panic that has been lingering. A higher pitch - a new sound bowl - makes the rug underneath me feel like a fluffy cloud. Floating, gliding across the skies, the sound lifts me higher. A lower tone brings in extra warmth and grounds me back down to my roots. It's only in places like these I can wholly accept myself, all of my flaws included. There's no weakness, no bitterness here. Only here can I allow myself to be fully me.

A harrowingly loud cacophony of dissonant sounds snaps me out of my meditative state.

The mask. *He's here.* The killer is right here.

He smashes two sound bowls - one with each hand - into Xen's skull. The snapping sound of bones and Xen's wailing woke everyone up. We all jump up and huddle together on the other side of the room. Aagje holds onto my arms.

"Xen, no!" Dimi cries out.

The killer repeats the same movement over and over, ramming the bowls into what's left of Xen's bloodied face. The rest of their body spasms erratically. The metal clanging fills the room as the blood spurts all over. Xen's screams become muffled and weakened. It's the same exact mask, the same posture, the same loose rags - it's *him*. My heart drums in my chest, and pins and needles flow through my shoulders.

With one more swing, their entire face pulverises into a puddle of dripping flesh.

Xen is dead.

I instinctively yell out: "Ivan Horvat!"

The killer turns around and faces us. Chills run down my spine. More screams around me as he walks closer to the group. To me. I ball my fists and crack my thumb.

"You killed Vera in this room, three summers ago. *Why*?" The words flow out of my mouth, there's no stopping it.

"Elo, who are you talking about? We need to leave, run!" Aagje tries to pull me out of the room, but I need answers. This might be my only chance.

"He doesn't speak, remember?" Esma yells out. "We need to get the fuck out of here!"

"No. I deserve answers."

"What the fuck, Elo, you won't find them here in front of a mute killer! Please leave with us!" Nils pleas.

"No, go. All of you."

"But Elo -" Aagje interrupts.

"I said go!" I yell out, as the masked killer takes another step in my direction. I push Aagje off my body, she's in tears. Her eyes are full of despair. Dimi takes hold of her and rushes to the hallway. The group follows my order and runs out, shouting and crying.

# Chapter 18

"Is this what you wanted? To lure more tourists?" I say in front of the killer, now that he is facing me, head-on.

I'm revved up, I won't go down without a fight now that I have him in front of me.

"Speak, you bastard, we all know you can!"

There's no reading his body language. All I can tell is that he is breathing deeply and tensing up his shoulders. The eyes coming through that awful mask are pools of black.

"I'm not scared of you!" No reaction whatsoever. He's just standing there. The way he was in front of our tents. It's obvious now that it was him.

I grab the pocket knife out of my shorts and with one swift move, I plunge it into his chest. I yell out my entire soul as I stab him. "This is for killing the only person who cared!" The knife penetrates the dirty, old black rags and sits there as blood spews out of his chest. But again, no reaction.

He pulls out the pocket knife and - before I can react - thrusts it into my left arm. A sharp pain shoots through my entire body. Then it dawns on me. The utter stupidity of thinking I'd get any answers. Or rational explanations. Or closure. As the stinging worsens in my arm and the blood gushes out, I realise I've failed.

I need to get the hell out of here.

In the blink of an eye, my entire stress response switches back on. What the hell was I thinking I'd do? Stab a massive killer to death with a pocket knife?

His hand goes into one of his pockets. He pulls out a massive old cleaver. *Oh fuck.*

He grabs my bloodied arm and drags me to the wall on the left. I scream out in pain and terror, hoping someone in the group will come back. He forces my hand palm onto the wall and as much as I try to wriggle out of his grip, it's no use. He lifts the cleaver. My heart sinks.

"Please, no, no! Wait!"

The weapon slides through my entire wrist, as if slicing through butter, and my hand falls onto one of the rugs. He lets go of me. I grab my arm with my other hand and stare at its gaping wound and rhythmic jetting of dark red blood. Tears muddle my eyesight and I'm light-headed. I think he's enjoying this, seeing me weep.

He lifts the cleaver again, but I finally force myself out of freeze and run out of the room.

My left arm is flopping along. I'm trying to outrun him and make my way to the landing of the pink marble staircase. I glare back and see he's running after me now; at a slow pace, but he's so much taller than me, it wouldn't take much for him to catch up.

No fucking way, I'm getting out of here.

I make my way down the stairs, followed by Horvat. I continue screaming in the hopes of calling someone's attention. With each step I take, I can tell I'm getting weaker. The salty sweat drops covering my lips remind me I'm still here. I'm finding it hard to keep my balance, so I grip the banister of the

## CHAPTER 18

staircase with my right hand.

A swooshing sound of air being broken rushes past my ears. The cleaver hacks into my last hand. It drops down onto the staircase. Despair fills my lungs, I cry out into the hallway. The red streaks of blood cover the pastel-pink stairs. I continue my way down until I somehow reach the main hall. Horvat is still right behind.

"Aagje? Dimi?" I try to scream, but a mere whisper comes out. I can't think through the pain anymore. It's crawling all over and inside my body. Where *are* they? I want to grab my phone until it hits me: I have no hands left. The tents. Maybe they went to the tents?

I push the main doors open with my elbows, as the pressure on my bones intensifies the shooting pains. The sunlight blinds me for a second. I try to yell, but no sounds come out anymore. My eyesight is starting to get blurry too.

This *cannot* be it. I'm *not* going out like this, not after everything I've been through. Fuck that shit.

I drag my legs into the direction of my tent, still followed by the killer. I'm not sure what I hope to find there, but maybe the rest of the group is waiting there to attack him altogether. That's possible, right? They wouldn't give up on me that easily. They're my friends.

I can see my tent now, only a couple more steps.

The peaceful greens and browns of the leaves and branches around me get covered in murky reds. *Don't stop now. Keep at it. They'll be here.*

A horrific pain hits my back. The cleaver. I look back and spot it being jammed into my lower back. The Buddha mask is staring at me once more. He's toying with me.

I fall onto my knees. My entire body starts shaking. I'm

starting to lose my eyesight as well. The agony I'm in is overwhelming my senses.

The killer walks past me and zips open my tent. What the hell? Is he going to let me live after all?

I inhale as slow as possible and yell: "Help!" with my last efforts, but not much more than a squeal comes out. My knees are about to cave in.

Don't be defeated. You've been through worse. This will *not* be it.

The killer comes back out of my tent. He's got something in his hands, but I can't make out what.

What does he want?

He bends down and goes on his knees as well, facing me. More tears gush down.

He pulls my mouth open with one of his hands, forcing it inside, and my entire jawline cracks and locks.

My healing stones. That's what he took from my tent.

He smashes the Rose Quartz inside my throat. I attempt to cough it back up, but he pushes it down. I try to keep my eyes open and not lose consciousness as the sharp edges prick my throat. Then he takes the Red Jasper and the Moonstone and jams them down as well. My gag reflex is coughing them back up, but each time Horvat just pushes them deeper down. I feel cuts in my throat and warm liquid running down to my clavicle. I start to throw up, but everything is blocked.

He's got one more stone. The Cordierite, my guiding stone. *Not this one.*

The killer smashes the stone against my palate and closes my mouth. He shuts my nostrils with his other hand.

I'm choking. On my motherfucking healing stones.

Flashes of light burst through my eyes.

## CHAPTER 18

Everything hurts – until nothing does.

## Chapter 19

**AAGJE**

Dimi is holding his hand in front of my mouth. We're all seated on the floor, peering through a small window. My eyes are glued to Elo's mutilated body. I can't believe she's dead. She and Xen. The killer, barely human, is moving in an animalistic fashion. There's a sense of curiosity in his posture, bending over and looking at her body. All of this feels like a fever dream, like I'm dissociating.

"Please don't scream, Aagje. We need to be careful." Dimi whispers, his voice broken by the tears running down his cheeks. Esma squeezes my hand, her mouth is wide open - but she doesn't make a sound. Nils is sitting in the corner of the storage room we are all hiding in, rocking his body back and forth in foetal position. The four butcher knives we took from the kitchen are lying on the floor next to him.

"The door is definitely locked, right?" Dimi asks Nils. He nods back, still shaking.

Dimi finally pulls his hand back. I try to breathe, but something inside me is blocking me from inhaling deeply.

"She had cancer." I let out.

"*What?*" Esma replies.

## CHAPTER 19

"She was in remission, but she had breast cancer. This was supposed to be" - my voice cracks - "a fresh start for her."

"Holy shit." Dimitar whispers. "I didn't know."

"It seems there's a lot we didn't know." Esma adds as she scratches her scalp. "What was she talking about earlier? With Vera and everything? She recognised the killer, the mask. Did she tell any of you about this?"

None of us were in the know. What other secrets was she hiding? She never did open up entirely, nor did she partake in the Circle of Trust moment. Then again, neither did I. I haven't exactly been honest about why I'm here, so the last thing I want to do is judge the person who's been like an older sister to me.

We spot the killer walking away, further down the trail, behind our tents. No haste, no fear.

"What do we do?" I ask the others. "We can't just stay here and wait for him to come back." I turn to Dimi. "This is when your military know-how would come in real handy, sir."

He takes a moment to think. "Xen's phone."

"What about it?"

"We need to go back to the sound bowl room and take their phone."

"Why? We all have phones." Esma frowns.

"They've got Milo and Josip's number. We can call them. Milo is the only one with a vehicle. We're stuck inside the retreat, have you *seen* that barbed wire? We need his van."

"If they're still alive." I mutter. "But you're right, it's worth a shot. We should go straight away, now that Mr. Namaste Slasher is off into the forest."

Esma agrees. "What's up with that Buddha mask anyway?"

"Perhaps he found his own version of spirituality, after living on the mountain on his own for years?" I ponder. "There must be a reason behind the mask. According to your story, his parents were extremists and spiritual in a dark way and stuff. Oh my god, are we being killed by the, like, Devil version of Buddha? Should we pray or something?"

"*Pray?* To whom?" Esma asks.

"To Buddha?" I have no idea what I'm saying.

"Well, I'd rather get us out of here first." Dimi stands back up. "If we don't get the van up here, plan B is to find tools to break through the barbed wire and the electric fence, the thing with that is: it looks like quite a modern installation system. I have no clue how to switch that off."

"The control room?" I ask.

"What do you mean?"

"Isn't there always some control room in the movies for shit like this?"

"Right. Probably. But let's get that phone first."

"Deal."

It's the first time I actually understand I'm scared. When Xen was attacked and we ran away, some kind of survival mechanism must've kicked in. Or shock? I'm not sure. But wandering down these vacant hallways - butcher knife in hand - on the way to the sound bowl room, not a sound around us, makes my skin crawl. Every step, every dark corner is a threat. Dimi is practically carrying Nils. Something took over him the moment we sat down in the storage room. He hasn't spoken a word since. The sun is shining fiercely outside, but somehow that makes the fear even more intense. Stuff like this shouldn't happen in broad daylight. There's no hiding away in the sun. Walking into the sound bowl room is supposed to be a signal to

## CHAPTER 19

relax, to unwind. Now it's giving death. Seeing Xen's body on the ground, with pieces of flesh and blood spread around the bowls, is so surreal that it looks fake. The rays of sun lighten the blood stains around us to an unnaturally bright red. Blood so vibrant I can't believe it's real.

"Are we sure this isn't some sick social experiment?" I wonder out loud.

"The fuck, Aagje? We're at a mindfulness retreat. How would killing people in front of our eyes be an experiment?" Dimi retorts.

"I'm sorry - I can't -" I choke up again. Dimi lowers his shoulders - Nils still attached to the hip - and softens his tone.

"I know. I'm sorry too, I didn't mean to snap."

"Well, if we really want to make sure this is real, someone could check Xen's pulse." Esma replies. How can she be so rational right now?

She takes a few steps towards the body and lowers into a squat. She takes Xen's wrist and waits for some seconds. She turns around, facing me, and continues: "Yup, definitely dead."

"How are you so matter-of-fact about all of this?" I have to ask. That throws her off.

"What else is there to do? We want to make sure this is real, right? It is. There's no pulse and this sure as hell isn't some dummy." She exhales slowly, her face even sterner than before. "Let me get their phone. Also, keep your knives at the ready, everyone. Just in case." Nils, Dimi, and I all stare at her in disbelief.

"What are you all gawking at? You think I'm cold, don't you? Calculated? Listen, I've seen death before. More than once. The only way to survive this is by keeping a cool head and dealing with the facts. We'll have time enough to mourn later, if we're lucky. For now, I'm sticking to what I know works. What, did you think I just *strolled* out of the cult?" I semi-expected Dimitar to be the rational, calm one. Turns out you never know how people react in extreme situations like this. And what they've actually been through.

"Found it!" She pulls the phone out of Xen's pocket and shows us. Nils' face lights up, and a sliver of hope is finally thawing him. "Hold on, let's see how - I don't know their code."

"Fingerprint." Dimi says, almost embarrassed for some reason.

"Oh, right, duh. Good thinking!" Esma replies. She takes Xen's hand and presses their thumb onto the screen. Seeing their arm being semi-stiff while being lifted disgusts me. "Rigor Mortis hasn't fully kicked in yet, we're lucky." She adds. *Really*, girl? Is that necessary?

"I'm in!" She sounds enthusiastic, as if taking part in an escape room game. I miss Elo's softer demeanor. I don't think she would've been this cold. I mean, fair enough, she was a bit sarcastic and distant at first, but she was opening up. She was real, pure.

"Can't find Josip in here. Perhaps he's in there under some nickname or whatever."

"Try Milo, he's more important anyway. He's got the van." Dimi is scanning me, I know he also doesn't get her attitude right now. Don't ask me how I know, I just feel these things. I always have.

"Milo, Milo - yes! There's only one Milo in there, so let's hope that's him. Do you want me to call him here and now, or should we hide somewhere else?"

"Good point." Dimi says. Why is that? "Killers often come

## CHAPTER 19

back to clean up the crime scene. We shouldn't stay here. He might be on his way back to this room for all we know." The sliver of hope in Nils' eyes vanishes again. The knife he's picked up starts shaking. Dimi looks at it and squeezes into Nils' shoulders. "We're in this together, Nils. All four of us. Nobody is-"

The main door slams shut. We all scream.

## Chapter 20

"No, no, no, no!" Nils utters in complete panic. "He's here!"

"Nils, don't shout!" Esma replies. "What do we do, people?" She quickly grabs the remaining three knives and passes them to us.

"We can't stay here." Dimi whispers. "He's at the entrance, we're on the second floor. So either we hide in another room up here or run down the stairs and make our way out if we hear him inside a room on the ground floor."

More clanging sounds at the entrance. I stiffen up again, the palm of my hand is starting to hurt from holding the handle of the knife so tightly.

"It isn't safe here." I speak up. "We shouldn't be in the house nor the tents. We need to run out, all together, when we get the chance and run down the mountain to one of those villages and get help. The people there can help."

"Can they?" Esma questions. "What if they're all in on this?" I'm not surprised she'd think like that, after having lived her entire life in a cult. "And another thing: how would we even get past the electric fence?"

Heavy, slow footsteps make their way up to the marble staircase.

"Shit, he's coming up to the second floor!" I bite the

## CHAPTER 20

fingernail of my thumb. "We don't have time to discuss. We need to decide, now!"

"Listen." Dimi sounds strict. "We stay behind this door. If he comes in, we all go at him with our knives. One stab each, no hesitation. He'll get an initial shock reaction, which will give us time to run down. If he doesn't come in, but moves past this room, we make a run for it the moment we hear him enter another room. Fair?"

We all nod, even Nils.

"Get ready." Dimi adds.

We all stand by the door frame. I can hear the air going in and out of my nostrils, my mouth shut tight to make sure I'm silent. I try to breathe through my diaphragm, the way I was taught back in music school, but it's jammed. It's the only thing I have to do right now, but I'm panicking because I don't know how to breathe. The breaths are so shallow, I'm starting to get woozy. Dimi signals me. He makes an exaggerated in- and exhale gesture with his hand. I follow his hand, thanking him.

The footsteps are heavy and arrogant. Each thud makes me flinch.

He's close.

Nils has his eyes closed, some inaudible prayer is forming on his pursed lips.

Even closer.

I glance up at Esma, who is no longer Miss Rational. She appears to be as nervous as I am.

Too close.

He's in front of the door.

## Chapter 21

The killer swings the door open.

We all instinctively jump at him, each of us stabbing him once. Esma stabs his right arm, Nils his left. Dimi goes for the stomach and mine lands in his ribs.

*Breathe, keep breathing.*

He doesn't react. Not even a sign of being hurt, even though the blood instantly perforates his rags. He only twists his head left and right, calmly taking in all of our faces. When the Buddha mask faces me, I'm swallowed up into hell. There's nothing human behind those eyes. This is what true evil looks like. My hairs stand on end and I push down a painful swallow.

"Go, go, go!" Dimi shouts. Esma, Nils, and I rush past the figure into the hallway as Dimi holds him back. The killer is at least fifty centimetres taller than Dimi, but Dimitar looks determined. I sprint past them into the hall, bloodied knife still in hand. A horrific squeal echoes into the hall, it's Dimi's.

"Dimi!" Nils screams.

The three of us look back at the open door frame. Dimi stumbles out, holding onto one of his arms. He's been stabbed. He's lost his knife, apparently.

"Keep moving!" He orders us. Nils rushes back. It's *his* turn to carry Dimi. The killer moves into the door frame and stands

## CHAPTER 21

there, agitated, breathing heavily. "Move!" Dimi repeats.

We all fly down the staircase, Dimi's grunting behind me is unbearable to hear. Some of my long blonde hair is stuck onto my face, because of all the sweat. It's dripping down my back as well. Ew, not the sweat. When we get down to the atrium of the building, I spot the killer on top of the staircase. He's getting closer.

"We need to move faster!" Esma commands.

"I'm fucking *trying*!" Nils grunts, still holding onto Dimi.

I turn back and help Nils out, so Dimi can latch onto both of our shoulders. Esma smashes the main door open and we all make a run for it, into the bright sunlight.

The scenery clashes with what's happening to us. All the peaceful nature of this entire retreat means nothing anymore.

First, he's right behind us, not exactly jogging, but walking fast. Somehow we manage to outrun him once we reach the dining table. I keep looking back, but I don't see him anymore. Why wouldn't he run?

We move past branches, past our tents, past open fields full of barley. Fields of Gold. That used to be my mom's favourite song. The bright golden and light green blur into blackness as we head towards nowhere.

"There! The fence!" Esma points up at a steep little path, leading up to the fence.

"So what?" I say, out of breath. "We can't climb that!"

"Perhaps the electricity is turned off, you never know! We need to try!" Before I can rebuke her point, she takes off even faster and moves up the path. Dimi lets out a harrowing cry when we push him further, up the steep part.

"I'm sorry, Dimi, we've got you. Right, Nils?"

"Right. I'm not letting go of you." His first full sentence. Perhaps focusing on Dimitar has brought Nils back. The vacant stare is gone, he's with us again.

By the time we reach the top of the path, we're all drenched in sweat.

"Okay, thanks. I need a minute." Dimi drops down onto the gravel and sits down, heaving.

Esma throws a branch at the fence, but the instant surge of electricity confirms my fears.

"What if we tie a part of our clothes around our hands and feet?" She suggests, but there's a tone of despair in her voice.

"Esma, that thing is at least five metres tall. There's no way. At the gates perhaps, but they're on the other side of the retreat and they're even higher than the fence. There's nowhere to hold onto there." Dimi manages to say.

"There's *got* to be a way!" She breaks. Her arms droop, and she looks completely deflated. Tears flood down. "I didn't kill my way out of that damn cult to end up being killed inside some hipster jail!"

"*What?*" Escapes my lips. Why *is* she here, if that's how she describes this place?

"Fuck this shit! This will *not* be the end of us." A raw angry scream rolls out from deep within her. Coldness appears on her face once more. "I'm getting us out of here." That was a quick turnaround. "Here, come on people, let's hide under these bushes for a moment whilst I call Milo." None of us protest, because something is telling me the safest thing to do is follow her command. I quickly glance around the mountain, but the killer is nowhere to be seen.

We sit in a circle underneath some cooling bushes, next to the fence. My hot skin appreciates the momentary relief from

## CHAPTER 21

the sunshine. Nils takes off his white T-shirt - that man is more muscular than I thought he'd be - and tightens Dimi's wounded arm with it. This time Dimi doesn't scream. He gives Nils a thankful smile. Esma pulls out Xen's phone and rings Milo. We all sit in silence. What if he's dead too though? *Then what's next?* The dial tone doesn't sound too promising.

Then we all hear his voice. Esma jumps up with joy. "Milo!"

It slipped my mind that Esma speaks Bosnian, so she's able to have a full-on conversation with Milo. I try to understand what she's saying, but except for that horrific name - Ivan Horvat - and the mention of Eloise and Xen, nothing makes sense to me. God, Eloise. Why did this happen to someone so kind, someone who's fought for years to stay alive? The tears are back, but this time I embrace them. I needed a moment of rest, to gather my thoughts. Out of everyone here, Elo is the one I had the most respect for. I could tell she'd been through shit, but she was still open to getting to know me. I know many people her age look down on me for the way I look. She at least made an effort to look past her own first impression of me. There was pain and bitterness, sure, but there was a big-ass heart too. Whatever transpires here today, I will miss her. I will make sure she won't be forgotten.

Esma puts down the phone.

"Well?" Nils asks. "What did Milo say?"

"It was a bit confusing, in all honesty. His dialect was stronger than I'd imagined. It's that older generation, you know?"

"Okay, but - I mean, is he coming over or?"

"He is." She's hiding something. I'm sure of it. She could say whatever she wants, really, but we wouldn't be able to verify. Those moments of coldness make me a bit wary of her.

"When?" Nils shows a frustrated grimace. "Come on, Esma, tell us more."

"Sorry, sorry. I'm trying to word things correctly and remember everything. He basically said he is quite far off, but he can be here by four."

"*Four?* What time is it now?" Nils wonders.

"A bit past ten." I reply.

"Yes, he said he is turning around the van instantly and will make his way back up north to this part of Croatia."

Dimi chimes in, "What I don't get is why an old man would be driving around Croatia for that many hours? In this heat? Why wouldn't he stay close by?"

"I - I genuinely don't know. He said he would call the police, so they'll be here well before him."

That sounds a tad more reassuring, but this entire situation is giving red flags.

I want to ask her how we would know she is speaking the truth, but that'd only make the situation even tenser. I *need* to believe her, for my own sanity.

"How long?" Dimi asks.

"About an hour."

"That long?" Nils sighs.

"It beats waiting six hours for Milo though." She tries to convince him. "That's not all, by the way. He told us where we could hide."

"What do you mean?" I ask.

"Well, the house, the tents, and this entire terrain aren't exactly safe with Ivan Horvat wandering around."

"What other option is there then?" I can't quite follow.

"There's a bunker."

"What?"

## CHAPTER 21

"A war bunker, underneath the showers. He told me where to find it and how to open the lock. It's completely hidden."

We all look at each other and agree.

"Show us the way." Dimi says.

## Chapter 22

"Wait!" Nils says, right before we head out to the bunker. "Why don't we head to the gate and try to open it instead?"

"The gate at the other side of the premises?" I reply. "There's nowhere to hide on the way there!"

"Plus, we don't even have the code." Dimi interjects. "What if the thing blocks after three times?"

"Oh my God, like on my phone. I hate it when that happens. I can never remember my PUK code, the absolute worst!" I blurt out. The others gape at me in disbelief. "But yes, the gates, absolutely. That would be bad." I mumble.

"Can't we jump over the gates somewhere? I'd rather escape than cage myself in some old-ass bunker." Nils asks.

"I did a check the first night." Dimi lowers his head. "The entire grounds are surrounded by tall electrified gates. There's no way out without Milo or Josip's help."

"Why would you check on the first night?" Esma frowns.

"It's, it's -" He stutters. "Call it force of habit." I suppose the guy has been through some shit in the army over the years. He probably checks all the locks and what-not.

"Right." Esma doesn't sound one bit convinced. "So, it sounds like the bunker is our only option until help arrives."

"What if it's a trap?" Nils semi-whispers.

## CHAPTER 22

"Whose trap?" I ask.

"Milo's. Or Ivan's. I don't know, it sounds a bit too obvious, doesn't it? A safe place to hide? What if Ivan Horvat spent years living in that bunker and is waiting for us there?"

Damn, why didn't I even think about that possibility? Nils kicks a tiny stone off the path awkwardly. "Or Esma's."

"Excuse me?" We all look at her. "In what fucking world would I have anything to do with this?"

"You're the only one who can communicate with Milo in his mother tongue. Fine, perhaps it's a coincidence, but you said you had family here!" Nils continues, speaking up a bit more confident this time.

"I didn't say I'm family with a serial killer!"

"Right, but how can we be sure? We only met you yesterday."

"Are you kidding me right now? *None* of us knew each other before yesterday." She makes a valid point there. So does Nils though.

"You *are* a killer. You said so yourself." Nils looks her straight in the eyes, not letting her off that easily.

Esma's face turns bright red, tears shooting up in her eyes. "They deserved to die. You have *no* idea what I've been through. What they've put me through. Don't trust me then, do as you please, but I'm getting the fuck out of here and into that bunker."

"Wait, guys, please!" I interrupt. "We can't turn against each other. We have no choice but to trust one another. It's either that or run off on our own. There's strength in numbers." Seeing Esma this upset convinces me she's speaking the truth. I need to defend her before Nils pushes her over the edge. She glances at me and whispers: "Thank you."

"It's bad enough having some random big-ass dude chasing

us, we can't have tensions within the group now that we need each other."

"But -" Nils tries.

"No, Nils, enough!" I shout back, surprising myself. "Esma is the only one who speaks Croatian and -"

"Bosnian." She corrects me.

"Sorry, Bosnian. She's the only one who *understands* Croatian. When the cops get here, she can explain everything."

Nils bobs his head in silence. "An hour, you said, Esma?"

"Right. The cops should be here in an hour." She exhales the tension out of her system and lowers her tone. "Milo told us to wait in the bunker, the police will knock four times on the door. That way we know they've arrived."

"Four times. Okay. Thanks, Esma." Nils adds, apologetically. She doesn't reply.

"It's ten past ten now." Dimi suddenly speaks up. "The police should be here around eleven then. Lead the way?"

"Sure."

"I have an idea, everyone!" I blurted out, a little bit too loudly. "I'll make a quick reel to-" Dimi rolls his eyes at me. "Hey, wait! Don't be like that! I've got a big following, alright? Almost one million people on Insta and TikTok combined." That seems to shut him up. "I am going to ask my followers to find out whatever they can about Ivan Horvat and this place. Who knows, some people might have connections or work for the feds or something."

"That's - that's a good idea." Dimi admits. The others nod in agreement. "But be quick."

I take out my phone and open up the app. "Namaste, bitches! Listen up closely, I need your help."

# Chapter 23

**DIMITAR**

Esma guides us to the changing rooms next to the showers and opens up the second room. The entire walk up here was spent in complete silence. The tension within the group needed a moment to evaporate, or at least subdue. I kept scanning the area around us, trying to suppress the triggers from my military days. Not a single sign of Horvat.

"Here, the entrance is supposed to be underneath the floor."

"What do you mean? It looks like a bunch of normal tiles." Nils states.

"Hold on, I've seen this system before." In Iraq, I almost add, but they don't need to know that. I reach for the square light blue tile on the top right, lift it, and turn it to the left. A clicking noise is activated as I pull out the entire fake tile floor and place it next to the wall. I try my best to ignore the biting pain in my arm. I'll be fine. A massive concrete door with a coded lever shows itself.

"How did you -?" Aagje gasps. "Oh my God, this is the coolest."

Nils looks at me with - I hope, at least - admiration. Even Esma is back with a smile on her face. I don't need to lead this group the way I used to, but it sure feels nice doing something to give back hope to the others.

Esma points at the door with her knife: "Is that there the lever?"

"I believe so."

"The code is 1995."

"Wait a minute, isn't that the year the War of Independence was won?" Nils asks Esma.

"Yes. Perhaps they changed the code once Croatia became independent."

I change the numeric lock to display 1995, shortly followed by another click. The door pops open from the left. I try to lift it, but the thing is bloody heavy.

"Wait, let me help." Esma jumps to the rescue and does most of the heavy lifting until the entire door is opened. Dusty participles ascend all around us. All we see is a black shaft with a vertical iron ladder leading down into darkness. Great, my biggest fear is back with a vengeance: claustrophobia. This is the last thing I thought I'd do on a mindfulness retreat. From mindful walking in the forest to hiding underneath the earth in a bunker. How things can turn in a matter of moments.

"So, who's going down first?" I ask the others. "I'll go last, to make sure the shaft is closed properly and Horvat isn't around." That and I'm scared as fuck to go in.

"The last time you played hero you got your arm stabbed, soldier." Nils winks. "*I'll* go last." I get distracted by his sweaty bare chest for a moment, before shifting my view to Esma. I ask her: "Will you go first?"

"Sure." Not a moment of hesitation. She would've been great in the army, but then again it sounds like she's had to deal with battles of her own. "Aagje can go after me, then Dimi, and then

## CHAPTER 23

Nils?" She suggests.

"Just how tall is that ladder though?" Aagje peers down the square entrance. "I can't even see the end of it."

"Guess we're about to find out." Esma smiles, for the first time in what feels like forever there's some warmth behind those eyes of hers.

"Be careful, Esma!" Aagje pulls Esma close and gives her a hug. It's a relief to see how they're pulling together again.

"Right, that's it. In I go." Esma shakes both of her hands.

"What are you doing?" Aagje asks.

"Excess of stress. I do this when I'm anxious. It makes me feel more focused after."

"That's probably the Yang that is shifting through you." Nils adds.

"Likely. Anyhow, here goes nothing, people." Esma lowers herself onto the ladder and climbs down quicker than I had expected.

"Don't go too fast!" I yell at her. "Slow and steady wins the race."

"Fine, grandpa!" Her laugh echoes upwards, she's quite low already.

Then her body is swallowed up by the darkness. We can't see her any longer. A pain shoots through my arm again and my chest is tight too. I know all too well what this is.

*Rationalise it.*

It's normal to be anxious right now, you've got this. You've gotten out of these bunkers in the past. We'll make it out alive. In less than an hour, we'll be drinking Rakija in some random beach bar. I'm sure of it. I allow myself to experience the symptoms, I've gone over it with my therapist so often. I know how to manage it. Fear is an emotion, just like happiness. I don't need to label it negatively.

"Are you there yet?" Aagje yells into the shaft.

"Almost, I think!" A faint voice tells me the way down is far deeper than I would've liked.

"Dimitar." Nils suddenly appears right in front of me.

"Huh, what?"

"I can tell something is up. You're tense." His light blue eyes are gentle and inviting. Damn, this dude is fine.

"I will - I'm okay."

"You've done this before, haven't you?" He continues. I'll give him this much: he's quite insightful for his young age. Aagje is not paying attention to us, she's still peering down the entrance, waiting, holding onto her knife for dear life.

"Too many bloody times, Nils." I reply. "It's the exact thing I wanted to escape from." It's refreshing to be this honest around someone new.

"Well, whatever you've been through and seen in the past, you've always pulled through. This time won't be different. It's one guy chasing us. One simple guy." He has left out 'humongous' and 'built like a tank'. "There's not an entire army to fight against, Dimi. One. Guy." He pats his hands on my shoulders as he emphasizes those last two words.

"One guy." I repeat.

His eyes pierce through me. The fear ebbs away as safety takes over.

He whispers. "Can I - can I kiss you?"

I didn't see this one coming. Not this sudden anyway. But then again, who knows how long we've got left? I simply say "yes". He pulls my jaw towards him and puts his hand on the back of my head. As he inches closer, I feel my entire body reacting. I quickly lick my lips before his tongue finds mine.

## CHAPTER 23

His second hand grabs the other side of my head as he goes in deeper and more passionate. I haven't been kissed like this in - in months.

"Wooo!" Aagje lets out a supportive scream.

We both get so startled we let go of each other and stare at her.

"What are you doing, Aagje, don't scream! Horvat could be lurking around!" I sound sterner than I meant to.

"Whatever, I'm sure he'd get off on seeing the two of you snogging." She giggles. Nils and I do too. "I ship this, the two of you." She clicks her tongue. The three of us stand there like a bunch of teenagers, talking about high-school crushes. I'll take this feeling over what's ahead of me.

"I made it!" Esma's muffled voice reaches us.

"Guess I'm next then." Aagje sighs. She pulls out some type of deodorant and rolls it over her wrist.

"What's that?" Nils asks.

"My lavender roll. It calms me down." She inhales the smell slowly. "Be good, boys. Or not, you do you." She smiles again before her gaze switches into focus as she lowers her body onto the first step of the ladder, the knife shaking a bit in her unsteady hand. She looks up one more time and says: "Namaste, bitches! This better not be a fucking trap."

## Chapter 24

"I'll be right behind you." Nils assures me when I head down the iron ladder. He sensed I didn't want to go last, thankfully. I didn't mind him kissing me again either. Well, not when it happened. A large part of me feels guilty, just seconds after. Thomas only passed away a little over two months ago and here I am - kissing a way younger dude I have a summer crush on. I didn't even expect to be able to have this sort of attraction to someone else. But it happened. And it happened fast. I can't lie: there's something about Nils that drew me in the moment I met him. I mean, granted, that body and those blue eyes aren't exactly hard to look at, but it's this sense of safety and warmth I feel when I'm around him. Like I don't have to explain every damn little thing I've been through. We had a cigarette together before it was my turn to climb down. He doesn't usually smoke - or so he says - but it was an almost ritualistic moment of togetherness before going under.

The coldness of the ladder bar shocks me back into the now.
*Here I go.*

I had promised myself never to enter another war bunker after Iraq. I know where ladders like these end up: isolation, claustrophobia, and disorientation. Worse still: away from my husband. If I hadn't been down in that bunker, I might've heard

## CHAPTER 24

faster about the tensions that were rising in his base camp. I could've done something, maybe gotten him out of there. But by the time my team came back up, it was too late. He'd been shot two days before we got out of the bunker. Everyone knew; the corps, his family, our friends. Heck, even my own family that I'm barely in touch with received a call before I was able to answer.

One hour, I can cope with one hour. The cops will hurry up, they must know Xen. Also, hearing two people have been killed in their little town will kick their asses in gear, I'm sure they have nothing else to do in a peaceful place like this. It'll be fine. I'll fly home to Sofia and visit Thomas' grave first thing. Well, perhaps a couple of shots first before flying home.

My breathing is becoming more shallow, but I remain focused on the end goal: getting out alive. It smells overwhelmingly damp in here and the humidity is making my clothes moist. Every single rung hurts a bit more, my arm definitely needs to be taken care of pretty damn soon.

I hear faint noises, it's the girls. It can't be too much deeper than where I am now, which is complete darkness. I hate not knowing where I am. Hate it with a passion. Losing control is never an easy thing for perfectionists, let alone in an unknown environment. Darkness gives too much space for thought, for over-analyzing. *Be here, be mindful.* Focus on the coldness of the bars and the sounds growing stronger. Breathe in through your nose, hold, exhale through your mouth. Repeat. *Keep going*, get to Aagje and Esma. You've been through worse. Ignore the pain.

"Dimi? Are you almost here?" Esma's voice echoes into the narrow shaft. It's a welcome distraction.

"I am, I think I'm close!"

"Good, you're going to want to see this!"

I wonder what she's on about.

Then I spot the final couple of bars and the lit up concrete floor underneath. I made it.

Aagje and Esma jump up to me and give me a hug before I can take in the room around me.

"You were taking ages, we got worried!" Aagje says, sounding all worked up.

"Sorry, the arm was slowing me down."

"Oh, of course, I didn't even think about that. Not me being forgetful." Aagje smiles. "By the way, Dimi, where's Nils?"

"He should be on his way now."

I shout his name as loud as I can, the echoes rising higher and higher.

He doesn't reply.

## Chapter 25

**NILS**

Man, man, why am I always so impulsive? What if he doesn't want to speak to me again once I'm down there? Well, we *did* kiss, twice. I suppose he would've stopped me if he didn't want to go at it again. Still, the man is a widower. This is why I'm still single, I end up kissing people without thinking twice. And then they think I'm some sort of a player who kisses everyone. Eh, I guess they're right in a way. Don't fall hard and fast like you usually do, you know it won't last. It can't. I can't replace a dead man, a husband even.

Okay, okay, shake it off. This is not the time.

*Thud.*

I spin around and scan the hallway of the showers. I heard something. I'm sure of it. It didn't come from down in the bunker. It was too close –

*Thud.*

Fuck, what is that sound? I squint my eyes to look deeper into the hall. I can spot the showers at the back, but I don't see anyone. The only thing I hear is my heart beating frantically.

*Thud.*

That's it, I'm out of here. I need to move fast.

A sharp, swooshing sound rushes past my eardrum. It's a hatchet. I jump back, further away from the weapon. That was a close call.

The killer, he's back. My stomach drops, and instant fear takes hold. He's standing in front of the bunker's entrance, blocking me from entering.

"Nils?" A muffled sound emanates from deep down in the bunker. It's Dimi.

"Help!" I instinctively yell back. "He's here!"

Horvat slowly lifts the hatchet, whilst staring me down. What do I do? If I run, I might never make it into the bunker. If I stay, I need to fight this giant beast - and with *what*? The knife, I forgot about the knife. I left it on the window sill behind me.

The hatchet comes swooping down again. I duck down, turn a one eighty, and grab the knife. I stay down and lunge at Horvat's legs, stabbing his right foot.

Not a sound, not a grunt, nothing. He stands tall and indifferent. Does this thing actually feel pain? I pull out the knife as the blood squirts onto my bare chest and plunge the knife into his knee. This time it has an impact. Ivan Horvat stumbles forward and almost falls down on top of me, but I manage to roll to the left side before he hits the floor. That's the thing with this killer. He's powerful, sure, but I'm slender and faster. He's not the most agile of men. I jolt back up from the floor, the killer still lying down.

This is my chance.

I run past him towards the door of the bunker. Just as I reach the door, he lifts himself back up and walks towards me. How is this dude not limping?

I jump into the shaft and hold both hands onto the top bar. I look up and scream: "Help!" again when the Buddha mask

## CHAPTER 25

stares right at me from above. I need to close the door or we're all screwed. I stretch one arm towards the inside lever and try to pull it down as hard as I can. It's heavier than I thought. Why isn't it budging? Then I notice the killer is holding onto the outside lever, which is stopping me from closing the door.

"You fucker! Let go!" I scream out in despair. He's strong, I can't do this. *Come on, pull harder.* I can't give up, the entire group is counting on me. They can't think I'm unworthy. I can mean something for once. I yank the lever even harder, but he's winning. The hatchet lands next to my hand, missing by an inch. I won't stay lucky. I need to do something.

"Nils!"

I glance down and see Esma climbing back up.

"I'm coming, hold on! I'm almost there! I'll help!"

I slide my body to the right a bit, so she has space to climb next to me. I admit, I'm relieved she's here, touched even. This was a losing battle, but now we stand a chance. Esma makes it to the top bar of the ladder and reaches for the other side of the lever.

"Come on, Nils, let's do this!" We both give it everything we've got. Esma shouts something in - I am guessing - Bosnian at Horvat. No idea what, but it doesn't sound like polite small talk. The hatchet comes back down, slicing deep into my right cheek this time. I cry out in pain and let go of the lever for a split second.

"No! Hold on!" Esma forces my hand back up. "Pull, damn it, pull!"

The stinging pain on my face was the exact type of fuel that I needed. Go to hell, Ivan.

With a strength I didn't know I still had in me, Esma and I pull down the door and immediately lock it up.

We did it.

"The code, what if he knows the code?" I whisper to Esma.

"Let's stay here for a second and check if he tries to break the code."

"And what if he does?" I ask.

"Let's hope it doesn't get to that."

## Chapter 26

After waiting for what felt like forever and not hearing a sound, Esma and I made it down to the bunker. The moment I step foot on the concrete floor, I burst out in tears. Esma wraps her arms around me and asks: "Are you okay? Is this like a release of stress or - ? Is your cheek hurting a lot?"

"No." I manage to get out in between sobs. "Nobody's ever done anything like that for me."

"Like what?"

"Coming back for me, helping me." I've helped hundreds of foster kids over the past few years, but nobody has ever really returned the favour. "Thank you." I mumble. Esma's eyes are wide open, I don't think she knows how to react. Aagje and Dimi rush towards me now and we all lean in for a group hug, the four of us.

"Your cheek. What happened?" Dimi asks.

"He carried a hatchet this time. How does it look?"

"Bad." Esma blurts out. "Good thing it didn't cut down to the bone, but your entire cheek is pinkish red." Great.

"I swear it doesn't hurt as much as it probably looks like. It's a little sting, that's all." Lies, my entire head is throbbing.

It takes me a moment to register where I am. I glance up from the hug and notice the low ceiling and massive concrete slabs all around us. It almost looks like one of those hipster hotels in Sweden where they repurpose some old factory and charge mad money for organic olives and sourdough bread.

"Brutalism at its best?" I ask myself out loud.

"I know, right? It's giving Urbex." Aagje replies.

I walk into what I suppose is some sort of living room. There are grey sofas set around some round glass table, other than that the room is as bare as it gets. The wall lights give off a warm sepia hue, contrasting with the cold concrete. There are doors all around the room, I have no idea how big this place actually is. Everything appears clean, nothing about this place seems old or derelict in any way.

"People must've lived here recently." I tell the others. "It even smells as if there's some sort of air freshener lingering."

"Lavender." Aagje replies. "I know my scents."

"What if this is Horvat's lair then?"

"Somehow I doubt a serial killer would spray lavender around his home." Esma jokes.

"Hey, you never know. Dude is a mountain man, he might enjoy some nature around him." Dimi adds. He winks at me. Guess he won't be ignoring me after all, that's reassuring at least.

"Let's hope this isn't his home. We waited for quite a while, but he never tried to open the hatch, so I am guessing he doesn't know the code." I reply.

"Then whose home is this?" Aagje wonders.

Esma bites her lower lip. "Milo? Josip? Could even be Xen's for all we know."

"Have you explored the place?" I ask the others.

"No, we were waiting for you." Dimi smiles gently. "I would've come up there instead of Esma, but my arm –"

## CHAPTER 26

"Oh damn, there's way more blood! Why didn't you say anything?"

"It's okay, it started bleeding again because I had to put pressure on it when climbing down that ladder. I'll be fine."

"Fuck that, you need bandages and the wound needs to be cleaned up. There must be some type of a first aid kit in here, it's a war bunker. Let's look around." I suggest.

"The police will be here in about forty minutes. I swear I'm okay. You need help though, that cheek –"

"I'm not taking any chances. I don't want your arm to get infected or something." I reply firmly.

"Fine, as long as you let me take care of your face as well." *You can do all the taking care you want, Zaddy. Don't, don't say it out loud.*

I open the door to the far right of the room first, followed by the others. It's the kitchen, about half the size of the living room. There's an old oven and cooker in there, alongside a dining table for four with dark blue plastic chairs. Ah, the tackiness of the nineties.

"Look, people, there's cabinets!" Esma jolts past me and opens them. "I *knew* it!" A large cabinet full of pickled vegetables in glass jars proudly presents itself. "Us Balkan people always have fermented food somewhere stocked up." She takes some jars and distributes them among all four of us. "Who wants cucumbers? I've got - bell peppers and sauerkraut too!" We all instantly dig into the food. I guess running for your life makes you hungry.

"Oh my actual God, this is so lush. It's giving rural kimchi!" Aagje looks delighted whilst she passes everyone some forks from the kitchen cupboard.

"Okay, okay, people, let's keep it moving. Take the jars with you, we need to find the first aid kit. Try the other cabinets too." But we don't find anything else in there, just spices and herbs.

We step into another room, adjacent to the kitchen. It's a tiny storage room by the looks of it. Tons of screws, hammers, and other equipment are laid out properly. Whoever did this is more organised than I'll ever be.

"I can't!" Aagje says, standing behind me.

"You can't what?" I turn to look at her.

"Oh, sorry, it's these pickles. I can't cope. So damn good." I can't with this girl.

"There!" Esma points at a red tin box. "That's usually what they look like, right?"

I take it off the top shelf and have a look. A sense of relief rushes over me when I spot the disinfectant, plaster, and bandages. "This will do."

"Great!" Dimi's eyes light up. He opens up another door whilst the rest of us are still munching away and yells out: "There's a bedroom in here, maybe we can patch each other up here?" Bedroom, somehow that word makes me nervous. What I wouldn't do to be in a bedroom with that guy, damn.

"Why don't you girls look around for anything else that could be of interest whilst Nils and I take care of our wounds?" He can't be serious. He was in the military, he should know not to split up in situations like these. Although, that does mean alone time with him. I'm staying really quiet here.

"Like what?" Aagje asks.

"Like weapons, more food, any kind of radio or walkie-talkie."

## CHAPTER 26

"Why would we need that?"

"Check your phones." Dimi replies calmly.

Aagje takes out her phone and frowns. "No reception."

"Of course not, we're too deep down. Which is why the cops will knock four times on the shaft. Milo knew there was no reception down here. I'm sure of it."

"What if -" Esma's voice sounds raspy. "What if Horvat knocks four times and we all go up there, just to be chopped up into pieces?"

A moment of panic sets in for all of us. Dimi looks a bit rattled too. "Well, we all have knives." Dimi took a knife from the kitchen. "And we'll go up together. Four people with knives against one. We've got this, whatever happens." He pauses. "Actually, girls, you never know - perhaps you could look for some type of mace spray. Or any other strong spray, anything that could throw Horvat off for a moment." Aagje and Esma seem to agree. "Right, let's meet up at the main room, the living room or whatever we want to call it, in - say, fifteen?"

"Right. Be careful!" Aagje says before she and Esma head in the opposite direction and open another door.

"So, Nils, you ready? Come in!" I walk into the bedroom and close the door behind me. He looks straight into my eyes and I'm more nervous than I've been this entire day.

## Chapter 27

"Was it really the best idea to split up, Dimi?" I ask, for lack of anything else to say. My nerves are high strung, and he is seated at the small bottom bunk bed.

"We're locked inside, this is as safe as it gets, given the circumstances. Come here." He taps on the bed, signalling me to sit next to him. Why the hell am I this nervous? Looking at his muscular arms and giant pecs, I'm already turned on. On top of it, he has this chiselled jawline seamlessly flowing into a perfect buzz cut. Man, man, he's way out of my league. I normally don't really go for the gym bros or girls, or people, but something about his self-confident demeanour is so damn attractive. A green flag gym bro, what's *not* to like?

I sit down next to him. "This might sting a little, Nils." He puts a bit of disinfectant on a scrap of cloth and gently pats it on my cheek. The pain cuts right through me, alerting my entire nervous system. I try not to scream, but I can't hold it in. He takes my hand in his and says, "It's okay, I get it. It hurts like hell now, but it's for the best." The tingles I feel in my hand counterbalances the pain, mellowing me. "Let me find something to protect your skin." He rummages through the first aid kit and puts a large band-aid over my right cheek. As he covers it, he looks me in the eyes again. *Damn*, boy, he

## CHAPTER 27

knows what he's doing.

"Is that better?" He asks, still gazing deep into my eyes.

"I - uh, yeah. So good. Much better." I stammer, like the awkward fool I am.

He leans in, his hand still on my cheek, now slightly caressing it. He knows how to get me hard. We go in for our third kiss today, each kiss bearing more intensity and passion. This one takes away all of today's hurt and anxiety. It's a release of the surrealism that has been unfolding. I lean back to take a moment. "I should take care of your arm as well." I whisper.

"It can wait." Oh, he's definitely turned on as well. I can feel him pressing against me, he's packing. I put my hand on his crotch and look up at him. "Is this okay?" From what I can gather from his physical reaction, it's more than okay.

"Yeah, definitely."

I unzip his tight jeans shorts and lower my hand inside his briefs.

## Chapter 28

**ESMA**

"Are they actually having sex right now?" I blurt out.

Aagje giggles. "I mean, unless they're in a lot of pain from the disinfectant, it sounds like they are."

"I swear, *men*. Give them ten minutes alone in a room and they're at it." Fair enough. That might be a generalisation, but I don't exactly have the healthiest relationship with anything sex-related. I'll stay far away from that after what I've been through. We're in another bedroom - this one has two bunk beds - going through all the nightstands and cupboards, but we can't find anything of use.

"I wish we had reception down here." Aagje complains. "Who knows what my followers have sent me by now."

"Hoping to go viral, are we?" I wink at her, teasingly.

"Not the shade!" She teases back. "Who knows what kind of exposure this can bring? All the collabs!" She switches gears. "No, but for real, these followers are pretty hardcore at times. Imagine the stuff they could dig up on Ivan Horvat." We walk out of the bedroom, the two boys are obviously still going at it. We crack up, they're not even *trying* to be quiet.

"Right, what about that door?" Aagje asks me.

## CHAPTER 28

"I'm not sure, this place is starting to look like a labyrinth. How many bedrooms have we walked into by now? Six?"

"Seven, if you include the sex dungeon over there."

"Ha, seven. I'm not even sure where the living room is from here. All the walls, floors, and ceilings look alike. Big-ass pieces of concrete everywhere." I flinch.

"What's up?"

"This entire place is starting to give me the creeps. The grey is so oppressive."

"I feel you, Esma, it's not exactly giving welcoming vibes. We'll be out of here soon enough." She looks at her phone. "The police should be here in like fifteen minutes or so." That sounds comforting.

"You're right, thanks."

"One more thing, Esma?"

"What is it?"

"I want to apologise for having a momentary lapse of judgment earlier on. I was so stressed up there and I -"

"It's fine, I get it. I speak the language, I have family here. I would've thought the exact same thing in your shoes." I'm not lying. I was offended for a hot second, but once I had some time to channel my thoughts, I got over it. None of us truly know each other, but we have to have trust.

"Thanks for understanding. We have to stick together, right? Us girls?"

"Always." I go in for a hug, because she's visibly upset about hurting me. "Honestly, Aagje, we're good." I can't always be this bad-ass, it scares people off. But then again, it was the only way to survive in the past. The moment I turn soft, I also become anxious. Because it's those exact moments, those seconds when you lower your guard, that people will fuck you over. I hope being vulnerable won't bite me in the ass.

There's one more door.

"Should we try that one?" I direct my gaze at it.

"Might as well, you never know."

I open the door and flip the light switch.

We both gasp and grab each other's hand.

*Ivan Horvat.*

## Chapter 29

*Ivan Horvat* is written at the top of a large notice board, above dozens of newspaper clippings. Aagje locks eyes with me, and we make our way to the board. I *knew* there were stories out there, just like I said before.

"They're all written in different languages." Aagje says.

"I know, hold on - I'm looking for any Bosnian or perhaps Croatian articles." I skim over the papers, but nothing. "I figured. Nope."

"Why are these all such tiny articles? There's no photos, no interviews." She leans in a little closer. "I don't recognise any of the newspapers either. They must've been local, unknown ones."

"How do you know?" I wonder aloud.

"Because I see one in French and one in German. I would have heard of them."

"Hold on, do you speak French and German?"

"Girl, I'm Belgian. My country is trilingual. I'm not saying I speak them perfectly, but well enough to understand. You're not the only multilingual one here." A little cocky wink. Fair play, girl.

"Fine, then what does the German one say?"

She takes hold of a little piece of paper on the left side of the board. "It's from 1997."

"Go on."

"Wait. Shouldn't we get the guys?"

"I'm not intruding on their disinfection session, no way." We both smile.

"Alright, I'll keep the clippings of the languages I understand and show them later. Hold on, let's see if there are any Swedish or Bulgarian articles." We both go over the board again.

"I'm not sure what Swedish looks like, they have a lot of weird vowels, right?"

"Exactly. Ah - here! This one's Swedish, or Norwegian maybe. All I can make out are the words 'Female tourist' and 'travel.' Doesn't matter, Nils will be able to understand. Do you see any Bulgarian ones? In all honesty, I mix up the Slavic languages."

"No, nothing. I'd be able to understand the context at least. I think that one's Albanian and the other Hungarian."

"No chance." Aagje smiles again. "So, let's check out the German one again." Aagje inhales deeply and shakes off whatever tension is in her shoulders. "Three tourists went missing on mountain Velebit." That's the mountain we are on. "It gives some info on who they were and their profession and ages, but nothing else."

"No info on Horvat?"

"Nope, nothing at all."

"Try the French one, it's a bit longer." I hand her the other article, hoping we'll find out more information.

"Let's see. 2006, a group of holistic leaders came up to the mountaintop as it is believed there is a unique vibration here that can lead to spiritual awakenings and healing. One of the leaders was Parisian."

## CHAPTER 29

"Did they interview them or?"

"They were all found dead. It was believed to be a cult –"

That word.

There's no way of knowing when it'll be flung back in my face. Shivers run through my body.

"And they – oh shit, sorry." She glances at me. "Are you okay? Should I not say that word or?"

"How – how did you know?"

"Your body language. I'm quite good at reading people." Her eyes are gentle and non-judgmental.

"I can see that. Scary. Anyway, avoid the word if you can, yes. I appreciate it."

"Okay, deal. Listen, they were believed to have committed suicide. They were almost all wearing –" I know where this is going. "Buddha masks. All except for one."

"He took it. Ivan. He must've taken the mask."

"Do you think he killed them all?" Aagje skims through the rest of the article.

"Hard to say. Would he put that much effort into making it look like a group suicide? How intelligent is he and what drives him?"

"Sorry if this sounds blunt, but I'm not interested in doing psychological profiling on that monster. For now, all I want to do is get us out of here and to safety."

"To the beach." I whisper.

"Girl, yes! I want to jump out of these damp clothes and into those turquoise waters, I swear! Esma?"

"Yes?"

"Who do you think kept these clippings?" Christ, for some odd reason I hadn't even thought about that. I was too intrigued by the clippings themselves.

"I don't know. Milo, Josip, Xen?"

"Do you think they were all in on it?"

I take a moment to think. "Elo *did* say she heard the two men arguing on the first night and they kept mentioning Horvat. It must be at least one of them."

"Would make sense, yeah. Xen also acted odd when we asked them about Horvat. They got all jittery. Why would they invite people here if they knew about this killer? I *really* don't get it. It doesn't make any sense. Perhaps all three are involved? But then why did Xen get killed?"

"Good question, Aagje. What if they were somehow trying to protect us, or one went rogue or something?" I take a glance at my phone. Shit, this isn't good.

"What's wrong this time?" Damn, can you stop reading my mind, woman?

"It's - the time. The police should've been here by now."

Her eyes fill up with fear. "Do you think Horvat got to them?"

"Let's not jump to conclusions. It's not the easiest dirt road to drive up to this retreat."

"These cops are from around here. They know the mountain, the roads." Anxiety sets into the tone of her voice. "We need to do *something*. I'm starting to get claustrophobic in this concrete box."

"You and me both. What if we -" I lean against the wall, but suddenly I stumble backward, and then a creaking sound breaks up the silence. What's happening?

"Holy fuck!" Aagje shouts. "Look behind you!"

I regain my balance and turn around.

"It's a hidden door."

## Chapter 30

"That's it. We need to go get the men." I urge Aagje.

"You're right. If this is another way in or out, we need to be together. Splitting up is always a bad idea. I'll close the door again first, to be sure no one can get in." I tap the same spot I put my hand on earlier and the massive - what looks like a fireproof - door closes. "How cool though." I add. "Can't wait to see what's behind it."

"Hopefully an exit past the barbed wire! We could get out of here right now. We did our part, we waited on the cops, but nothing happened. It's up to us now." Aagje speaks with determination.

I knock on the bedroom door and hesitantly say: "Eh, Dimi and Nils? Are you - done?"

Some muffled sounds come from behind the door. Oh come on, don't make this any more awkward. "Open up, please." Aagje stands behind me, hand in front of her mouth. "What are you giggling about?" I ask her, slightly annoyed.

"Sorry, it's your tone, it's - sorry."

Nils swings open the door, his long blond locks partially tied together. His beard is looking a bit scruffier than it did when I last saw him. "Eh, hey Esma. What's up?"

He and Dimi walk out coyly, like two caught teenagers.

"What's up? *Really*?" I ask. "What's up is that we found a room with newspaper clippings and a hidden door whilst you two were - *healing* each other."

They exchange shy looks. "Oh, that's great! Can you lead us there?" Dimi questions.

"Sure. Oh, Aagje, do you still have the Swedish article?"

"I do, wait!" She takes the crumpled paper from her skirt pocket and gives it to Nils. "There were other articles too, I'll tell you on the way there. What does this one say?"

Nils frowns and focuses on the tiny print. "It says a solo traveller, a female Swede, was found killed on mountain Velebit. She was - are you sure you want me to translate everything?" His look of disgust doesn't bode well.

"*Sure*, sure." Aagje responds.

"It says that human teeth marks were found on her corpse. Part of her stomach and, eh, buttocks, had been chewed off."

"I told you the other night that he's a cannibal!" Esma shouts out. "See, Reddit is not always wrong."

"I can't exactly say I'm happy you were right. Perhaps we should make a move to that door? I don't particularly feel like being his next meal." Dimi insists.

We head off towards the room with the hidden door. I glance at Dimi's arm and poke Nils. "You did well. His arm looks better. You must have some serious healing powers." We all laugh, it's a much-needed release of tension. Although I'm sure those men have released plenty.

"I try."

"He did well, he's very efficient." We all laugh again. Dimi continues: "With the band-aids, I meant."

"You did well too. My cheek barely hurts anymore."

## CHAPTER 30

"Do you need a post-healing cigarette?" Aagje teases.

"Don't even! I hope we can get the hell out of here and have a celebratory smoke." Dimi means business again, I can tell.

"So, this is the room?" Dimi peers around and brushes past the newspaper clippings. "I wonder who's been hiding in here. Do you reckon it's Xen?"

"That's what we were discussing as well." Aagje replies. "We can only hope that whoever put this together is out there to help us, not help *him*. It's been way over an hour, everyone. We can't wait any longer for the cops. Who knows if they're even alive at this point."

"Has it been that long?" Nils checks his phone and almost drops his knife in the process. "I lost track of time there."

"Sure, let's call it that." I reply sarcastically. "Enough with the chatting. Let's open that door." I walk up to it and hit the top left corner. The thick metal door opens once again, accompanied by some gasps.

"Wow, makes me wonder who actually built this place. This isn't any ordinary family bunker." Dimi explains. "Doors of this calibre make me believe this was some type of government hide-out."

"So, who's first?"

"I'll go, if that's fine with everyone. I went last before and, eh, it wasn't the best experience." We all agree with Nils. "Here goes nothing."

He hesitantly walks past the door into a dark hallway and stops before we can even follow him. "Hold on, people, there's another door on the left. I think it connects to the room you're in. Stay there."

"What? No, no, we're following you." Dimi says in a panic.

But Nils has already disappeared into another room. "What the hell? Come on, let's go after him!" We take off and run to the door on the left. Dimi swings it open. Nils is there, smiling.

"What the fuck are you smiling at? We said no more splitting up!"

"Easy Dimi, easy! Look, it's a one-way screen. We thought it was a regular wall."

We all walk into the room and spot the large window. He's right, you can see into the room we were in a mere seconds ago.

"The room with the articles must've been an interrogation room and this here would be where the detectives or psychologists followed the interviews." Dimi explains.

"Is it sound proof?" Nils asks. "Can you three go back in and say something? I want to know if someone could've been listening in on our conversations."

Dimi is unsure. "But then we're splitting up again and you know –"

"Just for a second. I'll speak too, let me know if you can hear me."

"I'll stay with you, Nils." I reply. I don't like the idea of him being on his own here either. "Don't even *try* to argue with me."

Dimi and Aagje run back to the interrogation room and stare at the wall.

"Oh, this is creepy." Nils utters. "We can see everything and they're staring at a wall. How does that even work? I've heard of one-way screen mirrors, but that wall is concrete."

"No idea, I'm not an engineer. Listen." We can hear Aagje and Dimi's voices, clear as day. "The acoustics are perfect here."

"Cool." Nils starts moving around nervously. "Okay, we

## CHAPTER 30

should stay alert. You never know, Horvat might know about these hidden rooms. Let's go. The others are coming back." Nils opens the door again and steps into the dark hallway. I am two feet behind him.

I spring up in shock. It's Horvat.

My neck.

Horvat's nails are scratching into my neck.

## Chapter 31

**NILS**

"Esma!" I shout, seeing Horvat grab her neck from behind. Garden shears are dangling from his belt. I leap on top of him, trying to free Esma from his death grip. There's no way anyone else is getting killed here. I attempt to reach for his arms, but this dude is strong. He doesn't even react to my attempts at freeing her. With one painfully effective elbow thrust, he pushes me off of him. I land on the floor behind them. My wounded cheek hits the ground first. A horrendous pain shoots through my forehead.

Dimi and Aagje have caught on, they're running towards the secret door. Esma is making horrific strangled noises. To my surprise, Ivan throws Esma - as if she were a rag doll - past the door, towards Aagje and Dimi. They all scream, toppling over each other. It's all complete and utter chaos. The killer smashes the door shut and locks it from the outside, pulling a lever I hadn't noticed before.

*Shit, shit.* It's him and me now. I stand back up, facing his back. The others are locked inside. I can make out some yelling and thuds against the door. I stare at Horvat's back and ponder for a moment on what my best bet is.

## CHAPTER 31

All of a sudden, he flips around. I do the same; time to run. He yanks my hair back and grabs the garden shears. "No, no, please! Let go of me, I won't tell a soul!", I plead, but I know pleading won't work. He probably doesn't even speak English. My neck cracks as he pulls my locks closer, and a burst of nausea sets in as he pulls me in even more. I spew some of those fermented vegetables, *great*. The sharp agony intensifies as he pulls even harder. Then I feel a release of the pressure. The shears cut through my hair in one swift go. My locks fall onto the floor. Not my fucking hair. I saved up *years* for those locks.

Then it clicks. *I'm free.* I jolt off into the hallway, not knowing where it leads, but not really caring right now either. I can easily outrun this fucker. Don't look back, go straight ahead. I hear heavy stomps behind me, but this is what I'm good at. *You're not getting me.* My breathing isn't as controlled as I'd like and my legs feel like jelly, but I'm moving quickly. He is picking up the pace too, though. He's catching up. *Come on, you've been a sprinter for years, don't let him win.* I continue my path, now almost completely in the dark. I pass some doors to my left and right. Screw that, I decide to go straight on.

A weak ray of sunlight creeps in, a mere couple of metres away. It's the exit. My way out of here. I can just about make out the contours of a large metal door. Almost there. *Come on, man, push on a little harder.* I let out a raw scream and fuel myself with adrenaline. Go faster. Horvat gets further behind. He's losing speed. *This is it.* I'm making it out. I'll get help for the others. The ray blinds me, but I let it. It warms my entire being. Everything we've gone through today, it's almost over. I can taste the freedom already. I take in a big gulp of air and let it run all over me. I open my eyes again. The door is two steps away. I'm getting out of this darkness. Perhaps I can run straight to one of the nearby villages and get help.

Take that, loser. I beat you.

My lungs collapse. Pain everywhere. What's happening?

I try to find an explanation.

Then I spot the pitchfork, piercing through my chest, blocking the door from closing. *It was a trap.* And I fell for it. That's why he slowed down. My heart is crushed. I was almost there. I go for a large inhale, but my lungs aren't cooperating. Blood spurts out of my mouth, and the metallic taste alarms me. I grab the pitchfork by the handle, aiming to release myself, but it doesn't budge. More blood gushes down from my bare chest. Horvat is behind me. I can feel his breath on my neck. He shoves his heavy boot against my lower back, pushing me even deeper into the pitchfork. I cry out in pain.

My eyelids are heavy. Don't. Close. Them. Stay here.

I can't. Stay.

# Chapter 32

**AAGJE**

I hold onto Dimi, he's still shaking and crying in my arms. The poor guy has lost it. Esma is still pushing and pulling everywhere at the door.

"It won't work." Dimi's voice is hoarse. "He's locked it from the outside."

"What kind of bunker is this if it won't let us out?" Esma yells out in frustration.

I need to keep my cool here. "People, take a beat. We need to regroup."

"But Nils -" Dimi protests.

"Nils is fast and he's smart. He could've made his way out."

"We don't know that."

"Exactly, we don't know what happened. Thinking only of the *worst-case* scenario isn't going to help us. Esma, come here." She pushes against the door with both hands one last time in vain, accompanied by a loud grunt, and joins Dimitar and me.

"We need to be rational. The police didn't come for us. Milo is hours away. What is our next move?" I ask the others.

"Well, we can't stay here, can we? Horvat knows how to get

in, we're caged mice in here, waiting to be killed." Esma makes a valid point. There's no safety to be had here.

"How about we try to go out the way we came in?"

"What good would that do, Aagje?"

"It'd at least get us out of this death trap, Dimi."

"And then what?"

"My followers. Perhaps they have info."

Dimi rolls his eyes again at the thought of that. "What could they have figured out that we haven't by this point?" Despair is kicking in, he's probably right. What else is there though?

"I don't know, okay? We can't stay here and wait forever. There's still at least three of us." Dimi looks hurt. "Probably four. We can fight back."

"Fight?" Esma cackles. "Really? Have you not seen that monster? He barely even flinched when we stabbed him. There's something unnatural about him."

"Or supernatural." Dimi adds.

"Who the hell knows? That article said this mountain has healing powers." Esma reiterates.

"What do you want to do? Throw your Chakras his way like a bunch of spiritual Power Rangers?" That came out a bit harsher than intended.

"I don't fucking know, Aagje!" Esma cries out. Her eyes are watery. "None of us do. But you're right about going back up. I can at least call Milo again."

"How can you do that without Xen's fingerprint?"

"I set up a new password the moment I got into their phone. How else would I have been able to call Milo in the first place?"

That's impressive thinking. "Clever."

"Thanks, I guess."

"Okay." Dimi interjects. "How about we run back up, Aagje

## CHAPTER 32

checks her socials and you call Milo. We stay right at the entrance in case the killer comes back."

"If Milo is still ages away, I can also call the cops. You know, in case they never got a call in the first place."

"Wait, do you reckon Milo never made that call?" I'm such a naive one at times.

"We can't be sure, can we? We need help, and fast."

That's set then. I am holding onto the last bit of hope I've got left.

We all make our way back up. My heart is pounding in my chest and I don't know if it's from excitement or fear. Probably a mix of both. I go first, Dimi is second, and Esma is last.

"We've got this, people!" I yell at the others, more to pump enthusiasm into myself than them, admittedly.

"Remember, Aagje -" Dimi says. "If the killer is there, get your knife at the ready when you push the door open."

So much for my enthusiasm; that died down quickly. "Right." Is all I can reply.

I'll be glad to see sunlight again, even though we haven't been down here for that long. It still messes with your brain. I keep climbing, one metal bar at a time.

"I'm almost there!" I glance back and see Dimi giving me a thumbs-up.

I tighten my grip on the knife's handle. *Don't drop it.*

I'm at the top of the ladder. The lever squeaks and protests as I push my entire weight into it.

"Do you want me to help out?" Dimi asks.

"No, it's moving. I've got this." I don't need your muscles for this one, sir. I can make my own way out. It's giving Lara Croft.

The sunshine comes flooding in, washing over us. I inhale the luscious smells of the mountain, before sharpening my focus to ensure Ivan is not here. It doesn't look like he is.

I hoist my body up and drop onto the changing room floor. I do a quick check of the different rooms.

"All clear, you can come up!" I yell at the others. The sound of a whole bunch of buzzing flies catches my attention. Dimi and Esma are by my side again. Esma has closed the shaft and changed the numbers on the numeric lock before heading my way.

"Do you all hear that?" I ask them. "Those flies."

Dimitar's posture changes instantly. "There!" He directs our gaze to a path behind the showers. "It's coming from there!"

We make our way past the showers onto the gravelled path.

A revolting scream bellows out of me. It's Xen, Elo, and Nils' bodies, piled on top of each other. Pieces of flesh are torn out of Xen and Elo's corpses. He's been eating them. I put my hand in front of my mouth and swallow the acid reflux back down.

Dimi runs to the bodies and checks on Nils. "No, please no, Nils!" He turns his body around, his entire chest is perforated, and there's dried-up blood everywhere. Dimi breaks down again, this time the despair in his howl makes my hair stand on end.

"His hair." Esma notices. "Ivan pulled a Samson on Nils." Dimi and I look at her in disbelief. "What? We were all thinking it."

## Chapter 33

I can't even *begin* to imagine what's going through Dimi's head right now. He had sex with Nils, like, half an hour ago and now he's dead. So is Dimi's husband. It's unnerving to see such a strong man crumbling to pieces. But then again I'm glad he can be vulnerable around us, he shouldn't have to put up a front. He's still standing by the bodies, but I can't. Seeing Xen and Elo's bodies, pieces missing, is too horrible a sight to take in. It appears Esma feels the same.

"Should we give him a minute?" Esma whispers to me, which is surprisingly empathetic for her.

"I think so. Let's stay close though. He's barely holding onto his knife. He could easily get attacked, judging by the state he's in."

"Right. Horvat must be around here somewhere. Otherwise, he couldn't have ditched Nils' body here right after offing him." And *there* she is again. Her vocabulary can be so direct at times. "So, let's stay alert."

I peer around me, we're close to the electric fence and there are bushes all around. Some large pine trees are providing us with much-needed shade. The summer sun is at its highest right now. The tents are a good ten-minute walk from here. We're out in the open, it's far too easy for the killer to spot us.

"We should find a hiding spot." I nudge Esma. "Do you think going back to the house is a dumb idea?"

"I think going anywhere in general out here is a dumb idea. All of this is Ivan's turf. His playground." Esma gazes off into the sky.

"How about Elo's tent? He wouldn't expect us in there, would he? It's nice and cool, those tents have great isolation this time of day."

"The tents? Sorry Aagje, but you must be joking. We'd be easy bait for him. He could pierce some garden utensil through the fabric and kill us all at once." Okay, dumb idea it is.

"Let's go to the far east side by the fence. You know, at the mountain peak." Esma and I turn our heads, and Dimi has joined in on the conversation. "There were thicker bushes by that side, and on top of it: if Horvat shows up, we can smash his body into the electric fence. It could kill him." He sounds calm and collected again, but I'm afraid his facade is back up.

"Not too sure if *anything* can kill him, but yeah - worth a shot." Esma replies.

We all walk whilst constantly looking around, butcher knife in hand, towards the top of the mountain. The wind is picking up here, the faint breeze from earlier strengthened by the height. For the first time, I notice some orange and red trees, maybe bushes, on this side of the mountain. The warm colours lead down to the beach, which feels further away as the minutes go by. I take in the waves in the distance and decide on my goal. Make it to the beach, wash everything that happened off me, and get the flying fuck out of here. About two hours ago there were six of us, by now the group has halved in size. It's complete madness how that much can happen in so little time.

## CHAPTER 33

I keep going through countless emotions, sometimes one by one, sometimes all at once; fear is certainly the paramount one, but sadness and anger are right behind. I need to do *something*. Right, the followers. By the time we nestle underneath some thick bushes in close proximity to the barbed wire and fence, I take out my phone.

"Can the two of you please keep a close eye around us? I'll quickly check which replies I've received."

"Aagje, not to be rude or dismissive, but shouldn't I call Milo and the police first?" She's getting used to me being more sensitive than her, I'd like to think. I appreciate the way she worded that.

"Oh, absolutely. Go ahead. Dimi and I will keep watch." Dimi nods at my suggestion.

Esma picks up Xen's phone again and dials Milo. The dial tone keeps ringing, but without an answer this time. "He's not picking up." She tells us.

"It didn't cut you off though, so his phone hasn't been stolen or smashed or whatever. That's a good sign." Dimi sounds hopeful, no idea how. "He still has battery too. He'll call you back."

"Unless he's part of all of this." I reply.

"Let me call the cops instead." Esma refutes. "They *have* to pick up. Give me a second, I'm looking up their local number." Seconds feel like minutes, any moment could be our last. It's tiny moments of silence like this when I realise how much tension there is in my body. I stretch wide and crack my spine and neck. Part of it is liberating, but there's too much heaviness left locked in my body.

"Got it!" She shouts. Dimi orders her to shush. "Sorry, sorry." The dial tone doesn't lead us nowhere this time around.

The cops pick up almost instantly. Dimi and I have a moment, he comes over and pats my back. "This could be it, Aagje."

"I hope so. What else can we do?"

"Let's wait until Esma tells us what's up first."

Once again I'm trying to pick out some words, but Bosnian is a complete mystery to me. All I can tell is that she sounds direct - this time it's a very welcome character trait - and adamant. It's quite a short call.

"So?" Dimi asks once the conversation is over.

"They're on their way. They'll be about fifteen minutes." I exhale a huge sigh of relief.

"What happened to the other ones that were supposed to be here, then?" Dimi questions her.

"Here's the thing: they never received a call from Milo. Nor from anyone else. Milo lied to us. I *knew* it." Esma's anger takes over as her cheeks turn red with frustration.

"That liar. He must know about Horvat then. Anyway -" I squeeze Esma's shoulder. "Great job calling the cops! They'll be here soon, that's all that matters. So, am I finally allowed to check what my followers have found?" I wink at Dimi, who doesn't know how to react.

"Of course, sorry about earlier."

I go through my socials and quickly become completely overwhelmed. "Wow, no way. I've never had this many views and reactions. I'm going viral!" Esma and Dimi snicker. Oh crap, I know how that sounded. "I meant - anyway, let me check my DMs."

I need a couple of minutes to skim through everything, most of them are messages of support, but some have done some *serious* deep diving.

"Well, anything new?" Esma asks impatiently. She's still

## CHAPTER 33

looking around for any signs of Horvat, as is Dimi.

"There's a lot of stories. More like urban legends. I'm not sure where to start."

"Give us a summary if you can. We don't have much time." Dimi sounds stern.

"Fair. There are more articles like the ones we have found. They all allude to foreign tourists going missing. I don't get how there are no local or even Croatian articles about him."

"Cover-up. Must be the local government trying to protect the region. They largely live off tourism here, it'd be a death sentence if the news spread." Dimi explains.

"*That* I get. I don't understand how the international press knows about it then. How could they if there's a cover-up? Anyway - there are tons of stories about the mountain itself too. The stories date back thousands of years, to days when people walked up Velebit to find healing. It is said there's a hidden source of water somewhere that can regenerate the body. The place became a holy site for pagans for a long time until Catholicism took over. It says it can't bring people back from the dead, but it can heal those who are hurt or sick." The two frown at me. "I know, that sounds a little floaty - but then again, we've all seen how strong the killer is. It'd be arrogant of us to dismiss anything spiritual when, frankly, we're at a mindfulness retreat." Water, healing. I remember now, my angel cards picked up on that yesterday night in the tent.

Esma glances up. "You're right. I've seen some weird shit through the years that can't or shouldn't be explained rationally."

"So, Xen must've known about the potential healing properties of Velebit? Otherwise, they wouldn't have chosen this location, right?" Dimi asks me.

"I mean, we can't exactly ask them now, but I suppose so." I pause. "There's more. There are stories about the locals who have spotted Ivan Horvat at the source - you know, where the water is - multiple times. They say he'd sit there, eyes closed, under a small waterfall. Even when he was a kid."

"So he *did* find his own form of spirituality after being rejected by his own parents." Esma interjects.

"How can you call someone spiritual when they kill people?" Dimi asks rhetorically.

I click on another DM. "Hold on - Here, look. There's a map."

The two lean in. "To what?" Dimi asks.

"To that water spot, the holy source, whatever you want to call it. It doesn't look far away at all. It's close to that little town, on the east side."

Dimi peers a little closer. "You're right, that's probably about a fifteen-minute hike past the fence." I can tell he's thinking about his arm. Those healing properties must sound enticing to him.

"This is all interesting and stuff, but our priority should be getting out of here alive." I focus on the matter at hand again. "It's no good finding some magical water if we're dead."

Esma startles and lets out a tiny scream. "The phone! Xen's phone. Someone's calling them." She says.

"Who is it?"

"Joso - oh wait!" Esma shuffles around nervously. "That's the diminutive for Josip. It's Josip! I didn't think of that earlier, but I bet that's why I couldn't find his name."

"Well, pick up already!"

## Chapter 34

"Wait! Pretend to be Xen, don't say too much at first and see what he has to say." Dimi suggests.

"Deal!" Esma picks up. We can all hear Josip's agitated voice, there's terror and frustration apparent in his tone. Esma says some silent "Uh-uhs" here and there. Josip is falling for it, I think. We're so lucky to have Esma by our side. Not only for the language, but she's also been the one helping out people when they need it the most. She might be a tough cookie, but you can count on her. A soliloquy flows out of Josip, accompanied by Esma's ever-widening eyes. I'm so curious about what he's saying.

Then she starts talking for what seems like ages. Dimi is worried and I can't lie - so am I. She whispers to us: "I told him it's me. I had to, I've explained everything."

Dimi reaches out his hand: "Can I?" he asks Esma. She hesitantly passes over the phone to him.

"Josip, it's Dimi here. We need a plan B. How do you deactivate the electric fence or open the gate?" How am I always the one who finds out what's been said the last? I'm itching for updates. Come on now, hang up.

When Dimi finishes the call, Esma starts talking straight away. "Josip knew. He fucking *knew* about Horvat. He's an investigative journalist and he's the one who's been hiding in the bunker. He wanted the government to take things seriously. You know, he's not even a cook."

"To be fair, he knows his food." I add, not sure why.

"Eh, right. Anyhow, he had heard all this talk about Horvat for years and wanted to finally find evidence. His boss doesn't even know about it, he's gone rogue to present the story. Now listen, he told me *not* to trust the locals. They're in on it."

"I'm not surprised." Dimi sighs. "Who else is?"

"He thinks most of the cops know. They turn a blind eye out of fear. He says they don't regard Horvat as human."

"Hold on." I interrupt. "If we can't trust the cops, then what do we do? They'll be here in like ten."

"He explained how to open the gate." Dimi answers. "The password at the gate is 0123."

"You're fucking kidding me. All that effort with the barbed wire and the electricity and *that's* the password? Genius. That's it? No other codes to crack or -"

"No, that's it. We can walk out of here. For good."

Something tells me it can't be that easy, but for now, I'll go with it.

"And then what?" Esma asks. "Horvat will notice when those massive gates open. I checked before and they don't have taxis or Ubers here."

"The horror." I shiver.

"Then we run to whichever village we reach first and -"

"No." Esma interrupts Dimi. "Josip said they could be in on it, remember? We need to run to some sort of highway down by the foothill of the mountain and when we see a truck or a bus or anything that *doesn't* look local, we can try to hitch a ride to the airport."

## CHAPTER 34

She would survive an apocalypse, that one. "Good idea, Esma." Dimi luckily doesn't object. I continue: "Right, let's open that gate and get the fuck out of here."

# Chapter 35

**DIMITAR**

I've been letting these girls down. I'm an embarrassment to the military corps, to be honest. Esma is the one who comes up with the right ideas. I blurt out random shit, hoping something will stick. I haven't been able to focus since I found Nils like that. Not only did I cheat on my husband in a way - or didn't I? - I seem to have some sex curse going on. Whoever shags me ends up dead. Great, future therapy bills: incoming.

I type in the dumb-ass '0123' code at the gates, so I can at least say *I* got us out of there. I need redemption, don't judge.

"Can anyone spot Horvat?" Esma squints her eyes. "I don't see him."

"Me neither. But I'm convinced he's not going to let us go without a fight." Aagje's voice is shaky and a tad bit out of breath from running to the gate.

"Screw that. We're getting out of here." I type in the code, and a tiny green laser light is switched on followed by a click. A huge sense of relief washes off my shoulders. I needed a win.

"It works!" Esma jumps up and down. "Josip wasn't lying!"

The massive iron gates creak annoyingly loud, practically *begging* to be heard, but at least they're opening. The moment

## CHAPTER 35

there's enough space between the gates, all three of us squeeze through it.

"I'll close it again, wait a sec." I tell the girls.

"No, we have no time to lose!" Esma pleads. "Let's go!"

"It'll take literally three seconds, I need to -"

Esma and Aagje's shrieks startle me; I know what that means by now.

Ivan Horvat is standing by the gates, on the inside of the retreat. He's staring right at me through that mask, holding onto his garden shears. Where did he even pop up from? And why isn't he running? I leap towards the gate call box and type in the code once more. The gates take a moment to react. Too bloody long. Horvat is stepping my way, nearing the gates. There's no urgency in his steps though, it's as if he doesn't even *want* to get to the other side of the gate. My chest tightens up, there's that feeling again. Like poison ivy writhing across my lungs.

"Dimi, come here! He's too close!" Aagje begs.

The gates react, they're closing. "Screw you!" I holler at Horvat. "We beat you, you fucker!" I duck down, grab a rock from the path behind me, and smash it into the gate call box with all my might. It breaks immediately from the impact. "You're locked in, freak!" I laugh hard and spit on his mask. Horvat thrusts his shears through the gate, but misses me.

"Enough with the victory dance, Dimi, let's get out of here!" Esma reiterates. I take a few steps back, head towards the girls and Esma grabs me by the hand. I look down at it, surprised. "Where is your knife?"

"I dropped it over there. We've made it out. We don't need it anymore." She replies nonchalantly. I glance back at Horvat, who is still standing there, shears through the gates, immobile.

"Something is telling me we better hold onto our knives for now." I say to her. They both pick up their knives sheepishly and take another look at the killer.

"Right, ready? We head for the nearest highway or some sort of bigger road, remember? I do suggest we drop the knives before hitchhiking. You know, not to scare off every single person." Esma semi-jokes.

"Agreed. Let's get the hell out of here." Aagje stares at the path in front of us. We have quite the way down, but we've made it this far.

We're safe. Then why am I clutching onto my knife?

## Chapter 36

We've come so far into our escape that the running has become rhythmical, almost hypnotic. We all keep the same pace and jog down, lower and lower, distancing ourselves from the retreat. I try to shake off the guilt. The guilt towards my husband for connecting with Nils so soon after Thomas' death. The guilt towards Aagje and Elo for not taking them seriously enough the two nights they saw someone standing by their tent. The guilt towards myself, for not being the leader I am supposed to be. I failed *so* many people, including myself. I don't even know where I'm running to. What kind of life is waiting for me? I can't move back into solitude. I *won't,* I refuse.

I trip over a pebble, but manage to regain my balance fairly quickly.

"Are you okay, Dimi?" Aagje asks.

"I will be."

I have no clue how long we've been on the move. It could be five minutes, it could be half an hour. Luckily enough, there is this gravelled path for mountain bikers. If we follow it down, we'll bump into a main road soon enough. Now and then some branches provide shade for us, but for most of the trajectory, the afternoon sun is burning our skin. This part of the mountain is far more colourful than I noticed when first going up two days ago. There are wildflowers with iridescent purple and pink tones, mixed in with deep orange mosses and bright yellow grass. It's a magnificent spot. I'm overtaken by the wild beauty of Velebit, appreciating it properly for the first time. I will not allow the darkness to overpower this vista.

I abruptly stop. There's no way this is possible. Aagje bumps into me and topples over onto a mossy patch of orange. "Shit, Aagje, I'm so sorry!"

She stands up and brushes the dirt off her knees. "It's fine. Why did you stop though? A little warning would be nice next time."

"The holy place." Esma answers. "Aagje, look."

A small, yet powerful waterfall breaks into the deep turquoise waters of a lake. There are trees all around it, circled up as if protecting the sacred waters. The flowers look different here. There's nothing wild about them. They're spread out alongside the edges of the lake, each more elegant and vibrant than the last. An impressionist painting would stand no chance next to the breathtaking purity of this place. My eyes are glued - entranced even - to the waterfall. Something takes over me, I can't quite describe it, but I *need* to go to that waterfall.

"My arm." I utter softly, afraid of disrupting the harmony of this place. "What if these waters actually heal people?" I ask the girls.

"Only one way to find out." Aagje smiles and strokes my back.

"I'll be quick, I promise." We should be safe here, we've been on the run for quite a while, plus Horvat is locked in to begin with.

Nothing could go wrong here, right?

## Chapter 37

"I wish I had brought my healing stones." Aagje sighs. "All my spiritual stuff is still in the tent."

"I'm sure we can get it all back." I say, not trying to sound like I'm brushing her off.

"The angel cards told me about this, you know? It showed me a flow of healing waters." Her eyes twinkle. I wish I had this much belief in those things. I look over at Esma, and something tells me she and I are not as spiritual as Aagje. Still, the waterfall is luring me in. I can't even properly put it into words, it's as if I'm being tugged involuntarily. Rationally, I'm aware that these healing properties can't be true, but there's something else at play here too. Exhaustion, perhaps. Esma, Aagje, and I walk past the first couple of thick trees towards a small clearing that leads to the lake. There's no one else around, we have the entire place to ourselves. A gentle gust of air soothes my sweaty skin, nudging me to dip into the water. We all put our knives down on the grass. Somehow, it feels so incredibly liberating to take a break from survival mode that it makes me emotional.

I take off my tank top, to which Aagje says: "Damn, I knew you were ripped, but that's next level!" I chuckle. There are many things I am insecure about, but my body is not one of them. I've trained for over half of my life to get into shape. I lower my jeans shorts, take off my shoes, and dip my toes into the water.

"And?" Aagje asks.

"It's cold, for sure. But with this heat, I'm not complaining! Are you two joining?"

Aagje nods and takes off her top and skirt. "By the way, some followers sent me more info about this place, in case you're interested."

"When did you get a chance to read all that?"

"What can I say? I'm a good multitasker." She nudges me with her elbow. We're about to head in when I flip around and notice Esma's sad demeanour.

"Esma? Aren't you joining?"

"No, it's fine."

"Anything you would like to tell us?" Aagje asks.

"No, well, yeah - I have issues with my body. I'm not comfortable taking my clothes off in front of people. It has to do with my past. But genuinely, go for it! I'll sit here, by the edge, next to these gorgeous flowers, and dip my toes in."

"Are you sure?" I prod.

"Positive. One thing though - don't take too long. I still feel a bit iffy lounging about like this. We need to make it to the road."

"Agreed, you're a hundred percent correct." I smile and go in for a hug. "Sorry about the sweat." I add self-consciously.

"You're good, don't worry. Go on then, get yourself some healing." She pats me on the back and bends over to pull off her shoes.

"So, miss Clairvoyant, what else did your fans tell you about this place?" I ask Aagje whilst we're swimming towards the

## CHAPTER 37

waterfall. Diving in felt amazing; this wave of cold, sweet water cleansing us. I give a little wave to Esma, who is playing around with some flower petals, her feet in the water.

"My followers, not my fans."

"Got it, sorry." I don't get it.

"It's been said that injured people have been coming here for hundreds of years. Those who were desperate and had tried everything came here, or were brought here by a spiritual leader, and got better."

"All of them?"

"I mean, according to the stories, yes. Another follower told me it's all about being intentional. If your Heart Chakra isn't open, it won't work." No pressure there.

I think we're about a five-minute swim away from the falls. The sound they emanate is getting more intense as we get closer.

"What else?" I ask.

"Huh?" Aagje puts her hand behind her ear, signalling she can't hear me.

"What else?" I repeat a little louder.

"Oh, right. This waterfall is giving fierce, so damn loud!" She cackles. Some lake water makes its way inside her open mouth before she coughs it back out. "Apparently you have to stretch your arms out horizontally, hand palms facing up. Then you close your eyes and open your heart." Cheesy, but I'll listen. "You have to speak to the water gods and ask them to heal you."

"Gods, plural?"

"Paganism, Dimi. They don't believe in one supreme all-ruling God."

"Any specific names I should mention?"

"I only know the names in Flemish, but I'm sure if you say "water gods," it will be fine." The falls are far more grand once you make it in front of them. "There, we've made it. I'll wait here. I don't want to interfere with your vibrations." I can't believe it has come to this. Thomas would have mocked me so hard. But then again, why the fuck not? What else do I have to lose? My dignity? Heck - I lost that ages ago. I wave at Esma again, to make sure she doesn't feel too left out.

"That's kind of you." Aagje shouts.

"Okay, wait here - I won't be long. I don't want Esma to wait for too long."

I swim a bit further until I reach some slippery stones covered in wet moss. I lift myself up carefully and take a moment to center myself. One step and I'll be underneath the waterfall. *You never know, this could work.* Give it a go.

I inhale deeply and step into the cold streams of the waterfall, lifting my arms horizontally. The jets of water are far stronger than I had anticipated, so it's a bit of a workout keeping my arms in this position. That water though; the smoothest, silkiest water that has ever touched my skin.

*Hello water gods, and eh – goddesses, what's up? This is new to me, but – I could use some help. My arm is hurting. I'm not entirely sure how this works, but I'd be grateful for your healing. Also, in case you mend broken hearts: be my guest.*

Can't believe how corny that was. The water feels warmer now. Perhaps I'm getting used to the temperature, perhaps it's something else. Unless I've gone completely crazy - which is definitely a possibility - the colour of the water has a golden shimmer to it. What the *heck* is this? I'm so out of my comfort zone with all this stuff. I should head back.

I swim back towards Aagje, who is giving Eager Beaver vibes.

## CHAPTER 37

Look, I'm learning with the lingo.

"So, so? Tell me all about it?" She splashes her hands against the surface of the water.

"I'm not sure what to tell you. My arm still hurts."

"Did you feel anything though?"

"Maybe. Let's go back to Esma first."

"*Fine*. Damn, I'm so curious now!" She splashes water in my face. "You tease!"

We turn around, so we can head back to Esma.

*No.*

No, no, no. Not her.

# Chapter 38

**ESMA**

They must think I'm such a weirdo. After everything that has happened, I can't even get over my own insecurities to have a plunge with them. A part of me wants them to persuade me more, but the other wants to feel safe. Safety, it's a big one. It's something I haven't had control over for most of my life and after what has happened at Zelena Nada, I'm not sure I'll ever be safe.

Cute, Dimi is waving at me, he's got the biggest grin on his face. No idea if he believes in the stories about the waterfall, but after seeing how Horvat gets up again and keeps on going, nothing would surprise me about this place. It's mad really how quickly you accept the most unreal situations once you're in the thick of it. I have yet to grasp that Xen, Eloise, and Nils are gone. Today has been a blur. I've kept on going, fighting and staying strong, but now that I'm here - plucking away at some orange flowers - I can tell how exhausted I am.

Dimitar is underneath the falls now, I hope he gets what he wants. They better come back soon, we're not entirely out of the woods yet. I make little circles in the water with my toes, staring at the ripples. I try to calm myself down, because I

## CHAPTER 38

sense the anxiety is bubbling under. I refocus on the water. There's something about turquoise that feels almost unreal, ethereal even. I spot some tiny fish hovering around my feet. It's the clearest water I think I've ever seen. I can even see the sandy bottom of the lake, even though it's probably a couple of metres deep.

I've made it to Croatia, finally. I remind myself of the fact that I made it out of the cult. For *years*, I didn't think I ever could. I thought I'd end up dead, like my best friend who tried to flee. Sarah also wanted to get to Croatia. She never had any family here, but with Bosnia being almost entirely landlocked, it appeared the easiest way to live by the beach somewhere was to choose Croatia. So, this one's for you, Sarah. We've made it. Now the next step will be going to the town hall and asking for my family's address. They might not even be legally allowed to give me any info, but I have to start somewhere. If that doesn't work out, at least I found one family member online who lives in Split. It's the rejection that scares me the most. If they found out what I did, and which cult I belonged to, they might think I'm still brainwashed. I couldn't blame them for that, but it's terrifying. Running from what I thought was home to find a new one, without knowing how it'll end up is so fucking scary. I deserve a fair shot at life, I've crawled my way through it for years.

A larger, dark ripple confuses me. Hold on, that's not a ripple. It's a shadow. My entire body tenses up. It's Horvat. His broad shoulders looming over me block out the sunshine.

He pulls me by the hair and brutally tugs me out of the water.

"Dimi, Aagje, help!" I shout as loud as I can, but they're not responding. I don't think they can hear me. "Help!" I yell even louder, but nothing. Healing waterfall, my ass. The killer makes me stand up, facing him. His breathing is slow and controlled, quite the opposite of mine. His hand moves towards the garden shears that are dangling on his belt. Oh, *hell no*. The gravel underneath my wet, bare feet signals me to run. I push Horvat, somehow thinking that'll make a difference, and run back to the path we came from. I bite away the pain of the tiny, sharp pebbles clawing into my feet. I knew I wasn't a fan of reflexology. Dimi and Aagje have finally noticed me. I hear their drowned-out screams, they're swimming back. I can't wait for them though, Horvat is already making his way towards me, inching closer.

All I can do is run.

I make it to the path that goes down to the foothill, perhaps I'll bump into some people. There was a small town not far off. I'll have to take my chances with the locals and hope they're not all psychos. I hear the impact of Horvat's massive body onto the path. He's not far behind. I pick up the tempo, screaming for help and letting out the frustration of the pain my feet are in. There's no shade on this part of the path, and the hot stones burn into the soles of my feet. Think of what you're running towards, your *family*. My breathing is too shallow, I'll need a break soon. Think of the Wim Hof breathing method. If he can breathe under ice-cold water, I can make it through too. How is this ginormous man behind me even keeping up? Stop thinking, just move. Move until you can't anymore. Fuck, he's getting close.

The shadow of the shears breaks through the sky, cutting into my lower back from right to left. I don't feel anything at first, but then the agony rushes through my body, all at once. It's unbearable. I flop down onto my knees. Another cut slashes through my upper back. The sound of my body being cut open

## CHAPTER 38

can't be real. It just *can't*. This isn't happening to me.

Wake up, get the hell out of here.

I kick my leg backward and strike Horvat's kneecap, knocking him off balance and he takes a couple of steps back. I push onto my feet and get back up, the pain is making me sweat even more.

*Go, go, get out.*

I try to run, but I can barely walk. Horvat walks behind me, seemingly in no rush. Then he pushes my bleeding back with his foot, causing me to topple over again. I crawl back up and turn towards him.

"You lousy excuse for a human being!" I shout in Bosnian. "Our families have all gone through the wringer, and this is how you cope?" He tilts his head, probably not expecting to understand me. "Yes, you dumb-ass, I speak your language." Then I get a desperate idea. "Perhaps, my family being Croats, you can let me live? I'm not a foreigner, you see? We were all part of the same land. I'm not here to mess up your mountain." He's frozen. Is he actually contemplating letting me go? I should've brought the knife. I could've stabbed him right here, right now. "Ivan is the name, right? I'm Esma." I continue in Bosnian. "My family used to live on mountain Velebit too. Perhaps you and I are even related? You know, I would *never* reject you." Horvat puts his hands over his head and starts shaking it. Is this working? "This can be a new start for you today. We can walk out of here together, nobody needs to know what you've done. We all make mistakes." The desperate words keep flowing out, pushing away the biting pain in my back. I blink a little harder, my eyesight is waning. Horvat shakes his head "no", then begins slapping his hands against the mask. I try to find my balance, but I'm wobblier than I'd like. I need help, soon. Horvat droops his arms next to his body, shears in one hand, dangling loosely. I can grab them if I move quickly. "Do you - want a hug?" I open my arms and carefully take a step towards him. He doesn't move. This could work. A twisted nerve in my back sends shooting pains down my legs. *Ignore it, you'll be fine.* I take another step in his direction. "I'm going to give you a hug now." I can't believe I'm doing this. My heart is beating so fast that my ears start ringing. I wrap my hands around his tall shoulders, lifting my feet so I can reach him. Everything about hugging the monster that killed my friends feels wrong, but desperate times, you know? His body relaxes into my embrace. I try to slow down my heartbeat, but I can't. He lowers his head and leans against mine. A smell of death, blood, and sweat pervades my nostrils. His musky, deep breaths touch my shoulder, it makes me shiver. *Reach for the shears, now.* I slowly lower my left arm, hugging him a bit tighter with my right arm to compensate. I move my arm down to his hand that's barely holding onto the shears.

*This is it. Do it, Esma.*

I grab the shears and stab him in the neck. Blood instantly spurts out. It stays stuck there. His body tenses, and I let go of him. No screams or signs of pain, but he smacks my face hard with his hand. I almost lose my balance, but I remain upright. Horvat is tugging at the shears.

This is my chance.

I walk down the path, whilst Horvat is staying put and struggling with the weapon. I jog a little, but each time my foot reaches the ground, the pain gets too overwhelming. He's not following me. Good, I've got this. I notice a little aged wooden sign at the bottom of the path, reading what I guess is the town's name. *Go a tiny bit faster, come on, you can rest after.*

## CHAPTER 38

I reach the sign and follow the turn.

*Houses*, I spot some houses at the end of the path.

I glance back and - to my horror - notice Horvat is walking towards me again. His stance is no longer calm, there's fury in his tread. I jog, screaming out in pain, towards the end of the path, which leads to some main street of a town. As I enter the street, I see some run-down shops and houses on both sides. Most of the houses look vacant, but some have fresh flowers and bushes in front of the entrance.

"Help, I'm being attacked!" I yell out in Bosnian. "There's a killer, help!" I drag my feet along the street and see some older people standing by the windows of several houses. "Help me, please!" One by one they close their curtains. My heart sinks. Horvat has made it to the beginning of the street, closing in on me for the umpteenth time. The shopkeeper on my right switches off his light and locks the front door. They know. They know about Horvat, they must do. Tears come flooding down. "You're all a bunch of cowards!" I let out between tears.

"Young lady?"

I turn around. A tiny old lady is walking my way. "My dear, what has happened to you?" She asks in Croatian. Then she looks behind me and spots Horvat. "Ivan." She whispers in terror. She knows him. I'm sure they all do. "What is your name?"

"Esma." Why does she need to know my name?

"Esma, you need to hide and call for help. My house is over there." She points to the far right side of the street. It's a small, wooden house that has definitely seen better days. "Run in there, lock the door, and hide. Get into my house now, the front door is open."

I agree, as I don't see any better option for now. I don't have the strength to keep running. The lady gives me a gentle nudge towards her house. The killer starts walking again. "Fuck, okay - I'll go to your house. Thank you so much!"

I wobble my way down to the house. *Don't look back.* The front door is open, just like she said. I walk into a dimly lit hallway, there's wood on all sides of the entrance. I take a quick look back and notice that Ivan and the lady are walking toward each other, like an old-school Western Showdown. She has no idea what she's walking into. Actually, perhaps she does, but frankly, I don't really care. I lock the door and walk into the first door frame to my left. It's an old-fashioned living room. No, not here. I stumble the opposite way into the kitchen, which is equally dated. There's old lacework in front of the thicker curtains and on the kitchen table. Slavic patterns are all over the wallpapers. I hear a loud scream coming from outside. I'm too curious not to look, so I make my way to the kitchen windows. I make sure I'm out of Horvat's sight though. *Fuck*, the curtains. I stained them with my bloodied hands. Oh well, sorry?

I hear another scream. I peer outside, preparing myself mentally for what I'm about to see. Horvat slices his shears through the woman's lower belly, her intestines drop out. A long trail of light pink bowels rolls out onto the street. She doesn't react, I think she's in shock. So much for protection. Not like I expected any, really. The shears are pushed into the poor lady's eyeballs. Blood spouts out of her eye sockets. I cringe and duck back down, I don't need to see any more. No, thank you. Actually, I've got to make sure he doesn't stroll my way.

I peer out again and look the Buddha mask straight in the eyes. My belly tenses up immediately. *Fuck*, he's spotted me.

## CHAPTER 38

Damn, that was a dumb move. I need to hide. I saw a large closet in the living room before. Alright, get past the kitchen and past the hallway. I drag my feet across the kitchen. I don't have any idea how I can still move, but I'm faster than before I entered the house. I push myself past the kitchen door, cracking my spine. Another nerve protests and numbs my right leg for a split second. Damn, it hurts *so bad*. Okay, get to that living room. I enter the hallway and pause a second to pull myself together. Take a deep breath.

Horvat crashes through the wooden entrance, tearing the door down with his body weight. I shriek and attempt to come up with a plan. Horvat rushes forward with a speed I haven't seen. He's *pissed* at me. I messed him up before, I shouldn't have tried him like that. He grabs me by the waist and lifts me up. All the wounds draw more blood, I cry out in pure torment. "Please, let go of me. I made a mistake. We all do, please!" He's not listening. My feet are dangling in the air. I have no power left in me to claw my way out. He takes me up the stairs at the end of the hallway. With each step, I have less and less fight left in me. I can't do this anymore. My head starts bobbing. My neck muscles are caving in. I want to plead for help, but even speaking hurts too much. We're almost at the top of the stairs. What does he want? A flash of my brother and parents shoots through me as we make it to the landing. *Hold on, for them.* He carries me into what looks like the primary bedroom. Oh, *please*, not this. "No, no, no!" I mumble, but he walks past the bed. A rush of relief washes over me, but I quickly realise things aren't over yet. I get carried to the windows, looking out onto the deserted main street. The woman's lifeless body lies in the middle of it. Now what?

*No way, they're here.*

I bang my fists against the window, a bolt of energy bringing me back.

"Dimi, Aagje, over here!"

# Chapter 39

**AAGJE**

"Oh my god, Dimi, look!" I spot Esma on the second floor. It takes me a moment to understand what's happening. An older lady's body was the initial shock. Now this.

"Fuck, Horvat is holding her!" Dimi cries out. "We've got to help her!" That eerie Buddha mask is piercing right through me. I'll never look at Siddharta statues the same way.

"Come on, let's go!" We bolt towards the house. I keep eye contact with Esma, so she knows she's not alone in this.

A loud crash snaps us out of our plan. Horvat has thrown Esma's body through the window, a million shards cutting through the sky and her skin. She falls onto the ground from the second floor. Both Dimi and I freeze. It's as if the entire world has stopped spinning. Tiny pieces of glass whirl into the warm summer breeze, catching the ray's reflection, almost blinding us. This cannot be happening again. The street seems fake, almost like a movie set. These things don't happen in broad daylight, right? I need to wake up. I refuse to believe any of this is real. One single tear reaches my lips.

Oh, holy fuck, she's standing up. Dimi and I lock eyes and make a run towards her.

"Esma, hang on!" Her entire face is full of blood and ugly cuts. There's still a glimmer of hope in her eyes though. No idea how, but she starts jogging towards us.

"Faster, Aagje!" Dimi shouts when Horvat bursts through the doorway. How on earth does that dude have yet *another* weapon in his hands?

I sprint even faster. We're almost at arm's reach. A tiny smile appears on Esma's face as we approach each other.

Then I know it's over.

Horvat swings a shiny hatchet into a semicircle before it cuts right through Esma's neck. Her head flies off into the air, there's blood spilling everywhere.

"Esma, no!" Dimi shouts out. Her headless body continues running towards us until it droops down on top of me and we both fall down. The blood from her gaping neck wound gushes all over my face. The sticky crimson red flows into my hair.

I scream a guttural cry for help. "Get her off me, Dimi!"

Dimi bends down to push away Esma's body. Then I spot *him.*

"Dimi, behind you! Horvat!"

Dimi looks past me. Something's not right. "Aagje, behind you, too!" A piece of cloth is pushed in front of my nose and mouth.

## Chapter 40

My mum is singing along to that Sting song again. "Fields of Gold" is blasting through the speakers in the living room, startling some tourists as they pass by our house in the centre of Ghent. It makes me cringe when she leaves the windows open and sings – or attempts to – like that. A teenage girl is taking a video until I shoo her away like the pigeons on our balcony. Only *I* am allowed to mock my mum, thanks very much. I know what she's doing. She loves it when I'm embarrassed, so she goes full throttle. It has become a bit of a game to her. "How far can I push my daughter until she caves?" Well, you are testing my limits. She has the biggest grin on her face whilst wailing along to Sting. She twirls around the kitchen, towel in hand. "Oh, come on Aagje, you know you want to join in!"

The final verse of "Fields of Gold" is playing in the church. I stare at her casket and imagine her dancing to it one last time. I wish I had joined in that day. Some random neighbour is patting my back from her chair behind me. Leave me alone. This moment is between my mum and me.

I can't talk about her to anyone. Not yet. She always pops up in my dreams. Every single night. Usually, it's that final moment on repeat. We're at the airport in Brussels on our way to Croatia. She is dressed to the nines, the way she always is when in public, whereas I'm wearing my comfortable travel sweatpants. The smile on her face fades. A mass of people disperse and start screaming. I hear gunshots. My mum jumps in front of me to protect me. I swore to myself at that moment that one day I'd go to Croatia to honour my mother.

My head is throbbing. Flashes of light burn into my eyes. Where am I? *Oh no*, this isn't right. My stomach clenches up aggressively and I hurl up the food from the bunker. The acidity mixed in with the smell of my sweat makes me nauseous.

I look around and sense pain in my wrists and ankles. I'm bound to a sturdy metal chair. I still don't feel like I'm fully here.

"Aagje, stay with me." I turn left and see Dimi. He's also stuck to a chair.

"Dimi? What - what happened?" The brain fog isn't going anywhere anytime soon.

"Milo happened." a voice to my right replies. Who the hell is that? I flip to the right. It's Josip.

"Josip? What are *you* doing here?" None of this makes sense.

"Keep the volume down, Aagje." He replies, staring into the semi-dark around us. "He could be here any second."

"Who?"

"Horvat. Or Milo. Or both."

"Hold on." I blink a couple of times, trying to adjust to my environment. "Can someone explain where we are and what's going on? Like, *now*?"

"Do you hear that?" Dimi bends his head to the left. "The falls."

"We're in a cave underneath the falls." Josip replies. "I've been here before."

## CHAPTER 40

"Right." I'm so lost. "What are we doing here then? With you?"

"I'm an investigative journalist. I came here to conduct research on the stories around Ivan Horvat."

"We know that; you told Esma on the phone."

"I did? Okay, sorry, my head isn't entirely clear."

"I feel you. Anyway, go on."

"I've been staying in that underground bunker for the last weeks, getting closer to the story. I needed actual proof though."

"You mean, him killing innocent people?" Dimi asks sternly.

"Well - if you put it like that, it sounds -"

"Yes or no?"

"Yes."

"You fucking bastard. You could've saved us all. Nils, Eloise, Xen, and Esma would still be alive." That baritone voice of his frightens even *me* right now. Josip looks terrified. A drop of water coming from the cave's ceiling touches my forehead. It makes me jolt.

"It all happened so fast. I confronted Milo the other night -"

"The argument. I heard you two fighting by my tent." I add.

"I was afraid you had heard that. See, the thing is: Milo is Ivan Horvat's father." Say what? Oh my god, the *tea*. "I finally had proof of that when I overheard them talking on the mountaintop the day before you arrived." So Ivan *does* talk. "I confronted him with all the stories and he decided the best reply was smack me in the face and bolt off. He said I was being ridiculous. He got extremely defensive. That says it all."

"Hold on, Milo - Milo is Ivan's father? Isn't he too old?" I ask.

"They only got Ivan when Milo was in his forties. Milo and

his wife had tried conceiving for years. The story goes that his wife went under the waterfall, because she was infertile, and nine months later Ivan was born."

"This crap again? It's a bunch of bullshit!" Dimi isn't having any of this. "I went under the waterfall, in some moment of weakness. My arm is still hurting like hell. There are no healing powers or magic or whatever people say there is. It's bollocks!"

"Then why would you even go under the falls in the first place?" Josip retorts.

Dimi stammers. "I - like, I said, a moment of -"

"Weakness? Do you really believe that? You have been running from a murderer all day, but suddenly you see a splash of water and you decide to chill out and have a dip before reaching safety. In what world does that make any sense?"

What is he getting at? Come to think of it, that was a really dumb move we made.

"What's your point, Josip?" Dimi asks frustratingly.

"That the waterfall has powers. It pulls people in, the ones who are deserving of healing. You didn't choose to go there, it chose you."

"Oh for crying out loud, magical waters? It's an old urban legend, nothing more than that!" Something in Dimi's voice doesn't sound like he is too convinced any more.

"That's not what this town believes."

"Fuck this town!"

"I understand the frustration."

"*Do you?*" Oh, careful there Josip, Dimi is about to snap.

"Well, perhaps I don't. Anyway, this town fully believes that Ivan Horvat is some sort of miracle." He stops for a second, checking if anybody is around. Silence. "At the beginning, the town thought the parents and their kid were freaks, they

## CHAPTER 40

were too much into their spirituality and all that. But then small miracles started happening. Ivan would heal sick animals at first, just by touching them. Then he would help out sick classmates, then the elderly. After the war, only the older generation stayed behind and they had all seen what Ivan was capable of."

"You do understand that everything you're saying sounds ludicrous, right?" Dimi interjects.

"How many times have you stabbed Ivan?" Josip fires back.

"Eh - I'm not - many times."

"How much of an impact did it have? How hurt did he get?"

There's silence for the first time between the three of us. The only sound in the cave is the occasional drip of water echoing around us. It's fairly dark in here, but there's still a bit of sunlight coming in through some cracks.

I speak up. "He didn't. He got back up as if nothing happened, time after time."

Dimi lowers his head.

"My point *exactly*." Josip continues. "Whether you believe in spirituality, black magic -"

"Those two things are completely different and it's dangerous to mix them up." I have to object.

"Sorry, fair. You've all seen that Ivan Horvat is not a normal man. There's something more to him. And that's what the townspeople saw too."

"So why would they allow him to kill a bunch of people, for years and years?" Dimi asks, he's back to sounding neutral.

"Don't you get it? There are hundreds of stories like this from places all around the world. He's regarded as the prophet on this mountain. As a deity perhaps."

"Sacrifices." I whisper.

"Yes, sacrifices. For all of mankind, people have sacrificed to their gods. To appease them."

"But still, innocent people. Usually people kill *for* their gods, they don't let the god kill. It doesn't make sense for them to allow random people to be killed in their own home." Dimi utters.

"I agree, but people are selfish. They got the better end of the bargain. These people would be healed, and live a healthy life until they'd die peacefully, no pain. Can you even imagine that? A life without pain?" I sure can't. "Having the security of having their entire family around them, in perfect health? These people had witnessed horrendous things. All of a sudden they were promised health, as long as the occasional sacrifice came along too. Honestly, I can't blame them."

"So, Esma was right. The entire town is in on this, including the cops. What about other towns and cities around here?"

"Don't ask me how, but the only people who know the full story are the ones living on this mountain. Whispers and urban legends were spread here and there, sure, but nothing major ever leaked."

"Then how did *you* find out?" I wonder.

"I've always lived in the seaside town next to Velebit. The stories that reached me as a kid had always intrigued me. There were usually plot holes in the story and each version was slightly different, but there was always a mention of these healing waters. It is said that only those who are worthy would find the falls. So nobody from other areas ever found them. I did, after years of searching. I went under the waterfall one day."

"And?" I prod.

"And I've been healthy ever since."

## CHAPTER 40

Dimi doesn't believe him, I can tell. "Then how do you explain my arm still being fucked?"

"Give it a day." is all Josip replies.

"Why us?" I ask Josip. "Why not some people from other parts of the area? Why would they go through all this effort?"

"Think about the five of you." Josip breathes slowly. "You're all survivors, aren't you? All in your own way. That's one element, I'm sure. The purer and stronger the heart, the better the sacrifice. I know Milo had a hand in selecting you. Xen was naive and believed Milo would know better, because he'd had a lot of experience over the years with spiritual retreats. They had no idea why Milo was so invested in selecting you people."

"What's the other element?" Dimi asks.

"I'm sorry if this sounds blunt, but none of you have families waiting for you." That one hits home. I had never even thought about that. We're all loners. We never went into detailed talks about our families, but from what I've gathered, Josip is right. Distant family members might get worried eventually, but in those first days: no one would care. Perhaps my followers would though, there's power in social media.

"And if they do show up-" An older voice continues Josip's story. We all startle and look up. It's Milo, walking towards us from a dark part of the cave. "You'd be surprised how easy it is to bribe people. Living a full life without illnesses, who could say no to that? Granted, some people still spread the rumours, but they were all brushed off as silly little sagas or hearsay at the end." What is up with his English?

"You look confused, Aagje." *Fuck, don't hurt me, please.*

"I get it. Playing the older driver with broken English instills more trust in tourists. That's one thing I have learned over the years. City people all assume we're simple, stupid even.

Malina -" I suppose that is his wife's name "and I are scholars, intellectuals. We've devoted our entire lives to the true faith. You're all about to become part of something far greater than yourself. It's about losing the Ego and stepping into your Higher Self."

That pisses me off instantly. "No."

"Excuse me, miss? *No?*"

"No, that's not how Spiritual Awakenings work. You are misusing spirituality to further your own gains. There's nothing 'greater' about any of this."

"Funny one, isn't it? People 'misusing' - as you word it- religion. There's always more than one side to religion and organised faith, Aagje. But you need to open up your eyes properly to acknowledge that."

This is all a *lot* to take in. What if they're completely wrong and this waterfall is one massive placebo effect? I want to get more out of him, but how?

Then it hits. Fatherly love. "Okay then, tell us more about your son, the prodigy."

Milo lights up the moment I speak those words. So fucking predictable.

"My Ivan is more than a son. He's the saviour of Velebit. He will save the three of you as well."

"Wait, what, so he won't kill us?" Josip asks, full of hope.

"Not exactly. He will take your physical bodies, sure, but your souls will be freed and become part of these waters."

"I think I like my soul *inside* my physical body." Dimi responds.

"That is *such* a western perspective." Milo laughs haughtily. What a prick. "Have faith in my son. He will set you free." As if. We need a plan before it's too late. But how can I get us out of

## CHAPTER 40

here when we're all tied up? Dimi is signalling for me to look at his hands, but I don't understand what he's trying to tell me. Milo continues his tedious rant. "You will be grateful very soon, trust me. Ivan!" He calls out the killer's name. We all tense up. I try to wiggle myself free from the ropes without Milo noticing, but I'm completely stuck.

Ivan Horvat walks into the cave, passes his father without even looking at him, and walks straight to the three of us. That mask freaks me out every single time. This isn't Milo's son to him, this is his god. He reveres Ivan. Milo even takes a couple of steps to the side and lowers his head.

I close my eyes for a moment. Whatever is about to happen, be here. Be smart.

The bloodied hatchet slides out of his long sleeve.

He's ready.

## Chapter 41

The killer lifts the hatchet, which is towering above all three of us. I have no idea who he is aiming for. I can only hope it's Josip. Sorry, not sorry. I want to fight back, but I'm left powerless by these ropes. The frustration weighs heavier than the fear right now. I'm biting down my own teeth, finding something to control.

Ivan swings the hatchet around and spins to the side. The weapon lands in Milo's stomach. Ivan grunts loudly, a voice filled with anger. I scream out of pure shock. I didn't see that one coming. Neither did Milo, looking at his facial expression. He mumbles something to his son, it sounds like he's pleading for mercy. This is the first time I've ever heard a sound from Ivan. He didn't even sound human.

"Aagje, Josip." Dimi whispers to us both. "Get ready to run."

"What, how-" I can't find the words. Too much is happening at once.

"Trust me. Run to the back left side of the cave. That's where we got in."

Dimi jolts up, shaking off the rope until it falls to the ground. He explains: "I started waking up when Horvat was carrying me towards the cave. I pretended to be unconscious and saw how he roped my hands. Easy to get out, once you know the

## CHAPTER 41

military tricks." He winks. I glance away from Dimi to look at the killer, but he's busy dealing with his father. He's got his back turned against us. Dimi goes behind me and loosens my ropes in a mere couple of seconds before heading toward Josip. He halts.

"Dimi, untie me please." Josip begs. It's obvious that Dimi is having doubts.

"Dimi, no! You're better than this." I chime in.

"He allowed our friends to be killed, Aagje." His lips are trembling.

"Do *not* stoop down to his level. I beg you."

"Fuck. Fine!" Dimi quickly unties Josip as well. We all stand together, glaring at the scene that is unfolding in front of our eyes. Why on earth would he want to kill his own father?

"This way!" Dimi yells a little too loudly. Horvat turns around, he's spotted us. Milo says something to his son, but Horvat isn't having any of it. He grunts again and plants the hatchet deep into Milo's forehead.

"Wow, *damn*. That's our cue!" I let out. We all make a run for it, heading to the back left side of the cave. There's a small opening that leads back up to the outside world. The sunshine blinds me for a couple of seconds, my head is still hurting from being drugged earlier. The waterfall stands proudly beside us. The sun is lowering, the hottest point of the day is behind us. We run as fast as we can, following the little trail next to the lake.

"Where to?" Josip asks in the midst of sprinting past the falls.

"Take us to a main road." Dimi orders. "We need to get help."

"Right, I got you. Follow me!" Dimi and I exchange looks,

let's hope we can count on this guy.

"Stay close to me at all times." Dimi whispers into my ear.

"Oh, I'm not going *anywhere*." I smile.

"It's giving attachment issues." Dimi jokes.

"What are you two blabbering about?" Josip turns around, continuing at the same pace.

"Oh, uh, n-nothing." I stammer.

"Actually, Josip, I've been wondering -" Dimi takes over. "If Horvat supposedly only kills - or sacrifices, whatever - tourists, why would he have killed this old lady by the main street of the town we were at?"

"Which town?"

"I forgot the name, it's like a fifteen-minute walk from here."

"What did she look like?"

"Like your typical older woman. I mean, her insides were splattered across the street and her eyes were stabbed. I didn't exactly study her facial features." Damn Dimi, that's cold.

Josip halts for a second, we all do. Great, I need a second to catch my breath. He turns around. "Did she wear a long black skirt with red Slavic patterns?"

"She did." I reply. "How did you know?"

"That's Malina. Horvat has killed both of his parents." Josip looks pensive.

"That was his *mother*?" Dimi double-checks.

"Most likely. Why now? Why would he follow his parents' instructions his entire life and then kill them both today?"

"Is that - are you asking *me*?" I ask.

Josip chuckles. "No, sorry. I was thinking out loud. I must be missing something."

"Hey guys, could we run while we talk, please? We're giving

## CHAPTER 41

Horvat time to catch up by standing here." Dimi observes.

We continue our journey down the mountain path. The lake and falls are far behind us by now. Luckily, the sunshine doesn't burn as much as it did earlier. My ankles do hurt, though, those ropes cut like a bitch, but we're here. We've made it out alive. The killer is nowhere to be seen. I hope he's still cutting his father up into pieces. I suppose situations like these *do* toughen people up. I get Esma and Dimi a bit better.

"Guys?" Josip calls us.

"What?" Dimi replies.

"What date is today?"

"It's Thursday." I reply.

"No, *date* - not day." Josip corrects me.

"Oh, right. Eh - July -"

"Twentieth." Dimi completes.

"July 20. I *knew* it had to mean something." Josip mumbles to himself.

"What are you on about?" I ask, breathless from jogging. We've slowed down our tempo by now, to make sure we can maintain it until we reach a highway.

"I've been doing my research and I've tried to link up all these fables surrounding the mountain. Today is the festival of Perun." I hate that he's waiting for us to ask for an explanation. I roll my eyes at Dimi who is still next to me.

"What does that mean?" I ask as neutrally as possible. Incoming mansplaining in three, two, one -

"It's the Slavic pagan festival dedicated to Rod and Perun." Why are those names familiar? The messages from my followers mentioned them, but I brushed it off as unimportant. There was too much info to skim through.

"Wait, *what*? My followers talked about Rod and other names.

They're Slavic gods, right? Why would that matter?" What the heck is he talking about now?

"Don't you get it, people? Rod was the god of - amongst other things - rain, pregnancy, and fertility. *Fertility.* Malina was never supposed to have children until she walked under those waters."

"God of rain." Dimi repeats. "The waterfall."

"What are you two heathens talking about?" I half-jokingly ask. I cannot be the only one who's completely lost. I thought *I* was the floaty one of the group. "Can we take a quick break, by the way? I need some air."

"Sure, Aagje." Josip agrees. We all decide to stand under some thick tree branches. "But let's keep an eye out for Horvat."

"Right, you two boys lost me there. Dimi, you were the one who said you didn't believe any of that bullshit."

"I don't, but that doesn't mean Milo and the other wackos don't. I'm trying to understand their reasoning. Horvat's reasoning."

"What if he doesn't have any rational reasoning? What if he's a deranged psychopath who kills for fun and ends up killing his own parents out of sheer joy?" I ask the others.

"Or what if the townspeople believe Ivan Horvat is Rod?" Josip interjects. "The Slavic pagan god. We were talking about deities earlier on, right? Well, today is the day Rod is celebrated."

"Make it make sense to me, I'm begging you." I'm getting frustrated here.

"If Ivan Horvat is Rod, or at least believes he is Rod, today is *his* day."

"And you've never made that connection before? What about

## CHAPTER 41

all those other years when tourists were butchered by him? Was it also on July 20? What makes this particular year so special?"

Josip's eyes are intense. His brain is spinning. He grabs his phone. "That's an excellent question, Aagje. Wait!" He scrolls down several articles and notes.

"Are you looking up the previous killings?" I wonder.

"Yes, why?"

"Check someone named Vera, three years ago. Eloise mentioned her." I'm not sure why I'm asking, but it must've meant *something* to Elo.

"Vera - Vera, ah, here! One article from the States read that she was murdered whilst holding a Zoom meditation class. July 17."

"Elo must've been in that class. Why the hell would Milo invite her to the retreat if she'd seen the murder? Isn't that making things unnecessarily hard for Milo? He must've known she was part of that Zoom class."

"Beats me." Josip admits. "He likes a challenge? Wait." What now? "A year later two German girls went missing July 18. The year after -"

"Let me guess, July 19." Dimi adds.

"Exactly. And this year all the murders happened on July 20. Today. It *must* mean something." He bites the knuckle of his index finger. "Yes, yes. I've got it!"

## Chapter 42

**DIMITAR**

I deserve a medal at the end of this day for staying calm. I swear, this dude is testing me. What magical explanation does he have this time?

"July 20, this is the first time he has killed on this specific date in forty years." Josip whispers. "Ivan Horvat turned forty this year." If he's going to throw a bunch of astrology my way now, I'm leaving.

To my surprise, it's Aagje who continues. "Forty, as in the mystical number?"

"Exactly!" Josip replies enthusiastically. "In Sacred Scriptures, Christian and pre-Christian - although hardcore Christians would never agree that the number was already a mystical one before Christianity -" Take a breath, dude. "Where was I?" My point exactly. "Right, forty years signify transformation, growth, and mostly: new life. It's the turning point. One task is finished, and another will start."

"Horvat is finishing his forty-year task by killing us and his parents." Aagje frowns. "Is that it, you think?"

"Might very well be the case. Whether or not Horvat is a god, I do believe that -"

## CHAPTER 42

"He's not." I reply. I can't stop myself.

"Or not, I think he believes he is Rod. Because of the way he was raised by his parents. Don't forget they were extremists. They brainwashed their own child into believing he is special."

"What is his next task then?" Aagje chimes in. "If this one stops after the first forty years of his life. What's next?"

"No idea. Maybe this is where it all stops. Completely. The killings, the healing, everything. Perhaps it all makes space for something new."

"Listen, I have to stop you there, Josip." I can't anymore. "I'm not saying you're necessarily wrong. Milo and the other Looney Tunes of the mountain may believe in all of this. I've seen crazier shit in my life. However, that doesn't mean *we* should. Our job, our *only* job, is to get to the nearest highway and to never, *ever*, come back here."

"You're right, Dimi. Sorry, I got carried away." Aagje realises. "A part of me needed to make sense of all the senseless killing." A tear forms under her inferior palpebral sulcus. *Fine*, I meant her lower eyelid. I wanted to sound smart for once.

"Guys!" Josip interrupts. "Look down there! I knew we were close. A highway!"

## Chapter 43

I came here to find out if mindfulness could help moving forward. After Thomas' death, all I had inside was anger. I'd burst out into these fits that would scare anyone around me. I scared myself too. I wouldn't hear it when my therapist - whom I was reluctant to go to in the first place - suggested some meditation techniques. It all sounded too Hollywood, too LA for me. Until the rage had become so strong that my mind had gone to a very dark place. I had nothing to lose at that point, so I tried out a guided meditation. That was the first time I had cried after his passing. Something clicked that day. I believe it was about a month after the funeral. The anger was a form of sadness, I didn't know how to deal with it. So when I received a DM about Zelena Nada, I was way more impulsive than I'd normally be. It felt like a lifeline was thrown at me. I never even doubted why I'd get a personalised DM from the retreat, signed off by Milo. I was naive in my blind mourning phase. That sick fuck took advantage of all of us. Nobody in their right mind would reply to a message like that. I would've removed it, considering it as spam. But that's the thing: I *wasn't* in my right mind. It's almost as if Milo had sensed it. How? No clue. All I know is that the five of us who made it here never even doubted why we were chosen. No clue what happened to those

## CHAPTER 43

two Belgian guys who were supposed to show up. Perhaps they were killed by Horvat as well. Why would there be a 'selection procedure' to start with, at a mindfulness retreat? We were made to feel like exceptional people, the selected ones. And it worked. I had let my guard down one fucking second, and I ended up here.

"Come on, guys, we're almost there!" Josip sounds like an eager boy scout.

I glance at Aagje, who is smiling through the fatigue. I know she's struggling, but she's a boss. I had underestimated her big time. She grabs my hand out of nowhere.

"It's over, Dimi. We're getting out of this place." A crack in her voice shows she's getting emotional. I want to reply, but I can't. We're not out of here yet. I'll smile when it's truly over.

The luscious trees on both sides of the path stop abruptly to make way for the highway at the bottom of the foothill. The end is in sight. About half a minute's run I'd say, and we'll be on the road. I can already spot two caravans zooming by. We'll have no trouble hitchhiking at this place. There's plenty of traffic passing by. Josip is still ahead of us, jogging at the same pace we are. He lifts his arm and shows us a 'thumbs up'.

Then Horvat appears. Of course he fucking does. He steps out of the woods, onto the end of the path. Anxiety kicks back in. Aagje screams - no idea how she still has a voice - and yells: "How did he get here before us?" I'm not surprised. It doesn't make any rational sense, but then again, none of this does.

We all stop.

Josip takes a deep breath and turns to us. "I'll stall him. I'm going to walk up to him. The moment he moves in my direction, you two run past me. Don't look back."

I'm speechless.

"Josip, no! You'll end up getting yourself killed!"

"I'll take my chances. He's not supposed to kill locals."

"You're not *really* a local though. Plus, he has killed his own parents, I don't think the rules apply anymore." Aagje retorts. Horvat starts moving towards us. I startle and stumble back.

"We don't have time!" I shout.

"Trust me." Josip begs. "Dimi was right. I could've prevented all of this. I was too obsessed with Horvat and all the stories. This is my chance to make things right."

"But -" Aagje interrupts.

"No buts, this is your moment to get out unscathed." I guess he forgot about my arm, but fine.

Before we get a chance to reply, Josip walks towards the killer. He starts speaking Croatian to him. I wish I could understand. From the tone of his voice, I can make out a sense of anger and determination. Careful man, Ivan has the hatchet ready at hand. I wish I could do more. We don't have any weapons on us anymore, there's no sense in bare-knuckled fighting that thing. There's no winning. We've all seen his strength, or a glimpse of it. Horvat deserves to die, but I'm not sure he *can*.

"Ready?" Aagje looks at me. This is so frustrating, I've never run away from my opponent. It's not *in* me. It's an act of cowardliness.

Josip is standing right in front of Horvat, still talking away. His little monologue doesn't rattle Horvat one bit though.

"Dimi? Come on!" *Fuck*, this is frustrating. If anything, I can at least protect Aagje.

I nod, *get over yourself*. We jolt to the side of the path. Aagje is in front of me. We're moving closer to Horvat and Josip, who for some miraculous reason is still not butchered.

## CHAPTER 43

"A bus!" Aagje yells at me and points to the left. "There's a bus further down the road!"

I see it too, some type of tourist bus.

This is our shot.

We run past the killer and Josip. Aagje jumps onto the road and waves her hands frantically to catch the bus driver's attention. The bus is still a couple of metres away. I turn my head and see Josip has been thrown to the ground. Horvat lifts his hatchet.

*Leave no man behind.*

A flashback of all the people that have fallen in front of my eyes over the years floods my mind.

I can't do this.

I bolt back towards Horvat.

"Dimi, what the fuck are you doing?" Aagje screams out, whilst still waving at the bus. "Don't be a hero!"

Horvat turns his head to the left and looks at me.

## Chapter 44

I latch onto Horvat from the back.

Josip yells at me, lying on the ground. "No, what are you doing? I told you not to look back!"

"I don't take orders from you!" I shout back. Horvat shakes his back, trying to get rid of me. My arm stings again; magical waterfall, *sure*. The hatchet is still lifted high up in the air. I jump up, letting go of Horvat, and reach for it with my right hand. *I've got it*. I flop down onto the gravelled path, hatchet in hand.

Horvat stomps onto my wrist with his heavy boot. I can hear all the tiny bones cracking. The pain is excruciating. I shriek out all the agony, I'm sure my wrist is broken. *I thought I had it.*

"Dimi, no!" Josip yells out. He stands back up, but Horvat smacks him right back down with his left hand. I wriggle the rest of my body, but the weight of his boot impedes me from making any moves. The shooting pains drain me, I'm losing my energy. I can barely hold onto the hatchet.

*Thomas' face appears. He's got a cute little smirk on him. He signals for me to come home. Perhaps this is it. Maybe I was meant to come here, so I could be reunited with him. I've got no more fight in me. I'm okay with this. A sense of peace flows through me.*

## CHAPTER 44

"*Hell* no!" Aagje shouts. She runs back towards me and bends down to my wrist. Horvat lowers his head and glares at Aagje, daring her to make a move. She's not perturbed, though. She grabs the hatchet from my hand and glides past me on the path.

"Aagje, what -?" I don't get it. I look at the bus, which is parked by the side of the road.

"Did you honestly think I'd leave you behind?" She replies.

Horvat releases his grip on my broken wrist and steps in Aagje's direction. I expect her to scream, but she doesn't. There's something different in her eyes. She's got battle eyes.

She swings the hatchet around above her body, flailing a bit. It's probably heavier than she realised. Horvat doesn't move though.

Josip is coming back to himself again. He's probably got a concussion.

"Aagje, careful!" He yells at her.

Horvat whips his head around, in the direction of the sound, and stares at Josip. He looks taken aback. Josip's eyes are full of fear. The killer lifts his heavy boot and stomps onto Josip's head. The cracking sounds followed by pieces of flesh and skin exploding onto the path make me turn away. Poor guy, he didn't stand a chance. As Horvat lifts his boot, I can see the remains of Josip's head. Pieces of his bloodied skull are still visible, but most of his head is a mushed puddle of grossness.

"Hey, Rod!" Horvat glares at Aagje, there's confusion in his stance. "Happy birthday!"

The hatchet comes flying down into his shoulder. Unsurprisingly, it doesn't affect Horvat much.

"Pull it out again, quickly!" I yell at Aagje, who looks confused. She's heard me. She struggles, but manages to pull out the hatchet right before Horvat tries to grab the handle.

Aagje takes a step back, imbalanced and with exhaustion written all over her face. I stumble to my feet, she needs me. My broken bones cut deep through me, but I can't give up now.

"Pass the hatchet to me!" I yell at her from behind Horvat's back.

"No, Dimi, you're hurt. *I* need to end this."

She swings the hatchet across the sky a second time whilst letting out an animalistic growl. "Namaste, bitch!" She makes two circles with the weapon, gaining speed. Her arm muscles tense up, her eyes grow fiercer. The third circle is aimed at the killer. Horvat jolts in Aagje's direction, his two massive hands coming close to her throat. Aagje screams out something in Flemish, her eyes fixated on the mask. The heavy hatchet makes its way down to Horvat's head and slices through his neck. Just like that. I stand in awe, motionless. Blood splatters on Aagje's face, and she refuses to close her eyes. The head rolls down the path, towards me. I snap out of it and leap towards Aagje.

Horvat's headless body stands, not moving.

"Aagje, fuck me, you did it." That is all I can say. We stand next to each other, staring at what's left of the killer who has been stalking us all day. His body caves in and drops down onto the ground. All of the pain, the running, and the fear are over with one slick move. I'm still catching my breath, grasping at reality. How did she even do that? None of us have managed to come close to hurting him, and she decapitated him with one swift move.

"Want to see what he looks like?" Aagje asks emotionless.

"I - eh, sure."

She drops to her knees and grabs the Buddha mask with both hands. She yanks it and pulls in all directions, but it doesn't

## CHAPTER 44

budge.

"I can't get it off. Can you help, Dimi?"

I take over and try to lift the mask with one hand. Somehow it's stuck to his head. As if it's glued down. "That's weird. It's completely stuck. Am I going crazy or does the mask feel like skin?"

Suddenly we hear screeching tyres behind us. We jump up and look at the bus taking off onto the road.

"That's fair." Aagje says. "I wouldn't want to pick us up after this bloodfest either."

We both chuckle. "What a shitshow. Should we head for the road?"

"But I want to see what that bastard looks like." She protests.

"Me too, but I can't tell where the mask ends and where his face begins."

Aagje frowns at me. "What are you getting at?"

I'm not exactly sure. "I - I don't know, but this doesn't feel like a mask."

"Hey!"

We startle and turn around. A middle-aged man with a long white beard and long, wavy hair has lowered the front window in his car. "Do you two need help?" He's got a thick Spanish accent.

Aagje looks at me. "He's not a local. That's good." She wipes off some of the blood on her face. "What do you think? Should we?" I give the mask one more pull, but it doesn't move one bit.

I take a glimpse at the number plate of the car. It's Spanish, exactly like I thought. "Let's go. Let's get the hell out of here."

# Chapter 45

**AAGJE**

"Would you like to sit next to me, in the front?" The Spanish man asks kindly. I peer at Dimi and decide against it.

"No, thank you. I'll sit next to my friend if that's okay."

"Sure, hop in." He looks unperturbed.

We drive off, leaving the body of Ivan Horvat behind. Dimi is holding firmly onto my hand, I'm not sure which of us needs the other the most right now. I still feel quite numb. I'm not sure where that strength came from, or if it was even really *me* who killed Horvat. Something or somebody took over. I've never used a hatchet before, so how could I even aim that well? The good thing is he's dead, gone. The bad thing is I have more questions than answers after today.

I gaze outside the window, the winding road is taking us down, closer to the turquoise waters I've been dreaming of all day. It's as if I'm in some sort of trance, it's giving dissociation.

Xen, Elo, Nils, and Esma. I say their names in my head a couple of times to make sure they're not forgotten the moment we drive off to safety. They deserve to be part of this in some way.

## CHAPTER 45

A distinct smell enters my nostrils. Something burnt. I look around the car to make sure the engine isn't overheated.

"Sir, the car, is everything alright?"

"You can call me Veles. What do you mean?"

*Veles.* Why does that name ring a bell? "Oh, right. My name is Aagje and this is Dimi."

"A pleasure." He replies.

"I smell something, like a fire. Is your engine okay?"

"Wait a sec - me too." Dimi replies, his voice full of worry.

"We're right on time." Veles says, looking to the right of the road. Something about his voice means trouble.

"For what?" I ask. I squeeze into Dimi's hand as a signal to stay alert. He squeezes back.

"The forest fire. Mountain Velebit will be forever changed after today. But then I'm sure Josip has already explained all of that." He sounds stoic now.

"You knew Josip?" Dimi fires back.

"Everybody on the mountain did. He meant well, you know. He was the last rebel standing, you could say. He knew very well he wouldn't make it out alive today. Some would call him a hero."

I test the car door next to me, but it's locked. We might need to escape. My body is amping itself up again, readying itself for a potential battle.

"No need to escape, Aagje. Am I pronouncing that right?"

He looks through the rearview mirror and puts on a big smile.

"Yes - yes, that's correct."

"I've scared you two, I can tell. Listen, if I promise to tell you the truth, will you promise not to escape or hurt me?"

Dimi whispers "no" to me. "We can't promise you anything. Tell us what you want to, and we'll take it from there."

"A man of his word. I like your transparency, Dimi. Military men are trustworthy men, so I hope you will give this an honest shot."

What the flying fuck is happening right now? How does he know Dimi was in the military? I'm too confused to speak up or say anything remotely intelligent, so I wait for Veles to give us some kind of clarity. Why didn't we stay with Horvat until we got rid of that mask? How did my body even get into this car?

"You two deserve the truth. So did the others of course, but things worked out the way they did because they were supposed to."

I hide my phone between my hands and look through the messages my followers have sent me. There was something about a Veles somewhere. I'll find it.

"Let me try to be clear. Eloise was the first building block of the last shift." *That's* being clear? This is promising. "The sacrifice of her teacher Vera led her here. She was the purest of the five of you." Well, *thanks*, I guess. "There is a certain order that comes with sacrifices." That word. Josip was right. "The innocent blood strengthens Rod the most. Eloise's blood was needed to drive the rest of you. Xen was an unfortunate mistake. They were almost part of divinity, but that's a risk I suppose Rod took as Xen was the only one that had gone through all the steps to Spiritual Awakening."

"I have absolutely no fucking clue what you are on about, mate." Dimi replies. "If you want us to give you a shot, speak *human*."

"That is absolutely fair, Dimitar." Dimi never told Veles his full name. He looks startled. "Where do I start?" Divine mansplaining? I thought the worst was behind me, *great*.

"Most of what Josip told you is correct. He didn't tell you

## CHAPTER 45

the entire truth though. Josip was part of Velebit." How does this guy even know what exactly Josip told us? This is giving the Upside Down. "He's lived there his entire life. He's not from some seaside town, as he told you both. He knew what was happening on the mountain and didn't want tourists to keep paying the price. He wanted to stop the killings, like many others before him on Velebit. He knew that it was a suicide mission, though, but he had made his peace with that. What he didn't tell you is that most people on Velebit don't want this to happen every year, but they're too frightened to fight back. Their choice for the last forty years has been to live in perfect health and ignore the sacrifices, or fight Rod and *become* a sacrifice. They are good people, you know? These townspeople have been through a lot and on a human level one could say it isn't fair they've had so much to endure. On a divine level though, they were chosen. By the god Rod himself. Ivan Horvat is but a vessel for Rod." Dimi is trying *so* hard not to roll his eyes, I can practically feel his agony. "And I know you don't believe me right now, Dimi, and that is fine. Listen though, because tomorrow you will believe me. Oh, and check your arm."

He looks at his arm, glares at me and whispers: "What the fuck?"

"What is it?"

"Look." He turns around and shows me his arm. It's almost completely healed.

"I sped up the recovery process a bit, so you'd at least listen. Don't worry about the wrist either, it'll be healed soon." Veles says matter-of-factly.

"Well, I'm all fucking ears." Dimi replies sarcastically.

"When Milo chooses the sacrifices, he usually picks the right ones based on their spiritual levels. He knew that for the final year, risks were needed. The five of you were spiritual, but not Awakened yet. That means you are all more pure and less divine, which is what Rod needs for his transformation. Of course that also means you aren't completely open to what I'm telling you now. You are still very much rooted in your human form." I mean, he's not wrong there. I pride myself on being an open-minded woman. I don't shy away from spiritual or divine topics, but this is stretching it. Like, a *lot*. Where are my angel cards when I need them? Actually, where the fuck is my lavender balm?

"What does any of this have to do with the fire?" Dimi interrupts.

"My point exactly. You are all in such a hurry. Instant gratification. Your arm is healed, Dimitar, and not a word of gratitude."

"Eh, I - I don't know if - thank you?" Poor Dimi has no idea how to react. That makes two of us.

I keep scrolling through my messages in the meantime. If this dude really is more than a mere human, I'm sure he's well aware, but then again: he's not stopping me.

"You're welcome. The forest fire is the start of a cosmic shift. It cleanses the past years to make space for new life."

"Does that mean the people in that town are going to die as well?" I wonder.

"No, Aagje, the waterfall has protected them. They will all be evacuated in time. No more deaths."

I need to ask the following: "And Dimi and I? Will we die?"

Veles laughs heartily. "This entire story and it's still only about *you*, isn't it? You don't really care about those other people. That is why the shift is happening. People still haven't

## CHAPTER 45

learned. Don't you think we get exasperated too?"

"W-who do you m-mean by 'we', though?" I stammer.

"Keep scrolling, Aagje, you'll find out soon enough who I really am." A tiny smirk appears on his lips. Dimi looks at me in panic and asks: "Are you okay, Aagje?"

"I'm - I don't know, to be honest. Veles, are you going to kill us?"

"*Kill* you? I'm *protecting* you two. It's not my role to kill anyone!" He looks upset now. "I've been driving through these mountain roads for years, trying to protect the sheep and the tourists. Don't you get it? I'm on *your* side!"

There it is, the message about Veles. I gasp. This can't be true, none of this can. This must be some sort of madman who's been living in isolation and has lost his marbles. Horvat the Second, if you will.

"You've finally found the message, haven't you? And yet you still don't believe it." Veles continues. "No need to show, Aagje, I'll tell him myself."

"Tell me what?" Dimi's lips are pursed with tension.

"Who I am. I'm Veles, a Slavic pagan god. Go ahead, roll your eyes again." he teases Dimi.

Dimi looks at me to check if that's what my message reads. It does. "It's not that straightforward though. I'm the god of protecting cattle, travellers, and many other things."

"And the god of the Underworld." I add, with a tremor in my voice. Why am I just sitting here? I want to scream, fight, run, but somehow I can't. I *physically* can't.

"There's that, too. You *have* to know I'm here to protect you. Your only salvation is to be had in the Underworld."

Dimi's hand palm is getting sweaty, or it could be mine. A million thoughts run through my mind, but none of them give me an answer to my questions.

"Is that –" I swallow hard. "Is that where you're taking us?"

"It is."

## Chapter 46

**LANA**

My sister bolts into my bedroom.

"Can you knock? Seriously, how many times have we gone over this?"

"Not the attitude." she pokes back. I swear, Tina needs to learn about personal boundaries.

"What's up?" I ask reluctantly.

"I wanted to show you something." She looks at my phone screen. "What are you up to?"

"Miss Curious." I smile. "I was distracting myself from all the shit that's going on in this house."

She sighs. Crap, I should be a little bit more sensitive, she's still too young to understand everything that's happening around us. Or at least, I *hope* she is. There's only so much I can do to protect her.

"Look!" I decide to play nice. "I was going through Reddit."

"Are you going down one of your dark rabbit holes again?" She teases me.

"I confess." I put my hands up in defeat. "But seriously, this story keeps on getting weirder."

"You know it's just a bunch of losers making up stuff, right?

They're basically making a Creepypasta, hoping to go viral. There's no proof of anything."

"Alright, Miss Expert." So much for distracting her.

"Sorry, go on. Is it still about those Croatian people?"

"Yes. Well, no, they were tourists. Five of them disappeared after the forest fires on that mountain Velebit."

"What's so unusual about that? There are forest fires all over Europe in summer."

"Wow, seems like you *really* care about global warming, sis." I say sarcastically.

"You know what I mean, how is that scary?"

"It's scary, because one of them was like this health and lifestyle influencer from Belgium who asked for help on TikTok. She said there was this killer who was stalking them."

"Oh, for real?" *Now* I've got her hooked. "So, what happened?"

"She was never heard from again after that last post. Her profiles aren't blocked or anything, it's like she - vanished. Some of her followers have made videos about this lunatic who's been killing people for years on that mountain. Some of them were trying to travel to the place and investigate, but the police have taped off all access, *supposedly* due to the forest fires."

"That sounds fishy. Let me guess, there are tons of conspiracy theories."

"Like you wouldn't believe!"

"What's the craziest one?" She asks. It's nice to have a little moment of innocent chat between us. Life has been far too heavy.

"Oh, there are plenty of crazy ones. One said that the killer was some sort of spiritual guru, killing them as sacrifices for

## CHAPTER 46

the nature gods or something."

"Always those gurus. He was probably some kind of charismatic cult leader." She smiles.

"Totally! Anyway, it's weird. They haven't found any bodies after the fires, but the people in the town who were living on the mountain were evacuated. None of them were injured, they were all in perfect health. How strange is that? A bunch of old people, but no one died."

"So it's a happy ending?"

"Well, for the townspeople, yeah. But nobody found those tourists. It's like they –"

"Vanished. I know, you said that. They'll probably pop up somewhere soon, living their best lives in Bali or something."

"Maybe." I'm not convinced. "Anyway, what did you burst into my room for?"

"Oh, right! Listen. We've gotten this crazy invite for a collab."

"We? As in, the two of us?"

"Yeah! It almost sounds too good to be true, but I checked their website and reviews and everything and it sounds legit."

She's not making any sense. "What are you talking about? Context, sis."

"I received this DM from a guy called Milo Horvat who runs a mindfulness retreat in the south of Spain."

"Tina, come on, that sounds like a scam already."

"I know, but the thing is: he's offering the retreat to us for *free*. We can fly into Alicante and his team will pick us up from there. It's at the end of October. He's seen our videos and he's a big fan of the way we talk about mental health. I suppose it doesn't hurt that we have a huge following. The only thing he requests is that we make content throughout the retreat."

"What's the catch?"

**ALSO BY ALAN SHIVERS: The "Europea Halls" Slasher Trilogy.**

**BONUS: Chapter 1 of "Europea Halls"**

# ALZBETA

It's one of those dreary, rainy Belgian evenings typical for January. Or, let's be honest, most of the year. The rain is violently hitting the window pane next to me in the living room. I notice some slight condensation on the windows, making it hard to see the forest outside. It's only just past ten, and it feels like the middle of the night. The wind is howling ominously outside, hitting the glass veranda ceiling with its sharp voice. I see these shadowy figures dancing, moving in an eerily elegant fashion. I realise they're only tree branches gently touching the veranda ceiling, but somehow, they still make me feel uneasy. Something about this night just doesn't feel right. Even though

## CHAPTER 46

I'm home, a part of me doesn't want to be here. I look back at the ceiling and notice a dark, humanlike shape. Its right arm points towards the large stained-glass door. I squint my eyes and try to make out if this is actually a tree branch. My mind must be playing tricks on me, well, I hope it is.

A branch violently hits the ceiling. I look up in fear, but I can't make out where the sound came from. The wind seems to become less intense, at least for now. I exhale. Trying to ground myself, I sigh through the house's silence.

My phone buzzes. I jump, glancing at the chat.

MIOLAA group chat
*Oliwia: You on your way, Alzbeta?*
*Lucija: We're waiting for you, girl! We need everyone here!*

Matej looks up at me with those big, expressive green eyes. He tucks a dangling strand of his sandy blond surfer hair behind his right ear. He has been sitting on the red velvet sofa opposite me for a while now. The silence is getting to be a bit much.

"Is it the girls?"

"Yes. They are wondering where I am. I'm supposed to go out with them tonight."

This is starting to feel like a huge mistake. Matej shouldn't be at my house. "Listen, Matej, maybe you should go."

I can tell he isn't really listening to me. He is looking through the stained-glass windows into the forest. I'm not sure what he is looking at exactly, as it's pretty much pitch black outside, and the condensation is becoming more apparent by the minute. I look outside as well for a second.

"Maybe I should. Alzbeta, I just want to make sure that we keep this between us. At least for now. Can you promise me that?"

A pang of guilt blossoms in my chest. In a way, I wish my parents were home so they could kick him out instead of me.

"I—I don't know. Lucija's your girlfriend. She's one of my best friends. She needs to know; I don't want to hide anything from her."

I wish I could tell him exactly how I feel, but all I feel right now is confusion. I've never been the eloquent type. I've never been a liar either though.

He glances outside again, lost in thoughts. So I do the same. I think back to when I first met Lucija, last September. I was immediately struck by her presence. She had just moved from Croatia into the dorms with us. Most girls need a while to acclimatise and observe before even daring to speak up. Not her though. She came in with this quiet confidence, this tall, red-haired girl with the perfect curls. She's the entire package, really. She just has this sense of cool—you can tell by the way she dresses too. Minimalist, she calls it.

I wouldn't call her cocky; she just seems to know who she is and what she stands for. She is one of those people you don't just want to be friends with, but need to be friends with. Magnetic might be a bit of a stretch, but I have definitely felt intrigued by her. I almost felt a sense of relief when we became close friends in such a short amount of time. We bonded over our love for anything vintage. I love strolling around the streets of old town Brussels with her, searching for the next little antique shop or looking up which flea market to go to next. Me, the small tomboy next to statuesque Lucija, roaming the streets. What I love about her is that she never makes me feel insecure. As much as I look up to her, I do have a sense that we're equals —all of us, really. I hadn't felt truly accepted

## CHAPTER 46

before. In the past, some people looked down at me for being small. Others kept telling me "I look so cute in that sweatshirt" in the most condescending way possible. But with Lucija, it's different. I snap out of it and look at Matej.

"Lucija is probably wondering where you are. You should leave."

"If that's what you want. Will you be okay here by yourself? This house gives me the creeps." He turns away, staring at the grand piano in the living room's corner, which has gathered dust. My mom keeps telling me I haven't practiced enough since we moved to Belgium, but I can't seem to find the motivation.

I notice his eyes are wandering off to the family portrait next to the piano. I guess it's not everyone's taste, these massive paintings with Baroque golden frames. "Ornamental," my mom would say.

*More like pompous*, I would reply in my head.

"Why, not used to luxury, are you?" I smirk, but instantly regret what I've just said. I should know better than to rub the family's mansion in his face like that. "Sorry, Matej. I didn't mean it like that. That sounded bratty."

"Self-knowledge is the beginning of all wisdom." Matej smiles faintly. I'm glad he can laugh it off.

"Just think about what I told you, okay?" He pauses. "I guess I'm off, then."

I look down and stare at the Persian rug that's like a fluffy little island creating much-needed distance between us. "Thanks for understanding, Matej. I'll see you at school tomorrow."

Matej nods. He walks up to me, and for a moment, I freeze. I think we both do. He takes another step in my direction, and I can almost feel the heat of his skin. The smell of his musky cologne mixed with the scented candles sitting on the mantle of the fireplace make me feel queasy. The dancing shadowy lights of the candles contour his angular face. As attractive as he might be, this light—or lack thereof—makes me want to take a step back. I suppose that would be rude. We decide to hug it out. It's not exactly a comforting hug. The moment his skin touches mine, I feel tingles running down my spine, but not the sexy kind.

My body is giving me clear signals that it is time for Matej to go. I walk him to the main gate. I am a couple of steps ahead, so that I don't have to look at him. The moment I'm about to close the gate, he looks at me intensely. I know there's a lot more he wants to say, but I have reached my limit for today. I can tell he's gathering up the courage to say something, but I don't give him the chance. I quickly close the gates and mumble, "See you tomorrow then."

I couldn't be more relieved when he finally leaves. In a way, Matej is right. This house has always given me the creeps too. The creaky floorboards, the massive Renaissance ceilings, the little cherubs staring down judgingly every time I enter the hallway. I guess in a way, this house represents a new start to my parents. When we first moved to Brussels a couple of years ago, I never would have thought life was about to change the way it did. We never really had this kind of money before moving to Belgium. Back in Prague we were content with our little apartment. Life was simple but easy. Definitely easier than life in chaotic Brussels. God, I miss Czech food.

The TV on the first floor starts playing loudly. I jump up. I thought my parents were out. I'm sure I saw them leave. Oh God, did they overhear our entire conversation? The unease I felt earlier on with Matej around has only intensified. My chest feels tight, and my breath is becoming shallower by the second. I shouldn't be here. Not tonight.

"Maminka? Táto?" They don't reply. I am wondering where I last left the remote. It would be so me to sit on the remote without even realising it. But then, how could I turn the TV on when I'm on the ground floor? I call out for my mom again. "Maminka?" My voice is shakier than a second ago. I decide to walk up the golden spiral staircase towards the entertainment room on the first floor. When I open the door, I see the TV is still on, playing a video of our family trip to Singapore. I look around the room to make sure no one else is here.

It's just me. I try to recompose myself and take in the details of the room. Lucija told me once that if you feel stressed, look for objects with the same colour in a room. According to her, it will rewire your brain or something. Green—I'm going for the colour green. Red popped up first in my head, not going to lie, but I need a positive colour to calm me down.

The first thing I notice is the green carpet on the pool table on the left side of the entertainment room. What else? The green ball on the pool table, obviously. The accent wall around the chimney is also quite green. Vomit green, my dad called it once. Succulents, green. My gaze turns to the tiled floor in front of me. There are some hints of green in the Moorish tiles too. My mom did well with those tiles. I love the way the pattern creates some sort of cosiness in an otherwise quite austere-looking room. Then I see it—the remote is lying on one of the tiles just in front of the TV. The Singapore trip. I am taken back to the time when my parents and I were visiting those lush gardens, all lit up at night. I try to stay calm and reminisce about that trip, but I am already mentally looking for a way out of this house. I pick up the remote from the floor and turn off the TV. I stand here for a while, my breaths shorter by the second. My chest is really starting to hurt. Is Matej playing a prank on me?

The TV on the second floor starts playing. I jolt, screaming. It's the same video. I can hear my own voice, talking about the meal I'd just eaten on that rooftop restaurant in the centre of Singapore. The sound comes from my parents' bedroom. Something in my body seems to take over, and I rush towards the second floor, tightly grabbing the railing of the staircase. As I arrive on the landing, I start second guessing my own actions.

*Should I enter their bedroom? What on earth is happening? Is it one of those weird electricity surges I've read about?* I hold out my hand, staring at the adorned door handle. *Just open it. What is up with you?*

I swing the door open and half expect to see my parents in a compromising situation, but there's no one in the room. I'm not sure if I should feel relieved or terrified. I try to play the colour game to soothe my racing mind and look for objects around the room, but I can't seem to calm down this time. Once again, the remote is lying on the ground, this time on the carpeted floor right in front of my parents' TV. When I pick it up, I hear the floorboards creaking on the third floor. I stay down for a second, making myself as small as possible. I stay in that position for a while, frozen with terror, waiting on the next sound. The creaking stops. I quickly stand up again and shut the door, locking it. My hands are becoming clammy as my palms slip off the door handle. I take my mobile out of my right pocket and try to send a text as fast as possible, but my fingers don't seem to follow my thoughts.

Alzbeta: *Matej, are you still here?*

## CHAPTER 46

No reply.

Suddenly, I hear footsteps right above me, coming from my bedroom on the third floor. I manage to stay quiet, but I can feel my heart is beating in my throat. My mouth is dry too, and it feels like my jaw is completely locked with fear. I look at my phone again.

MIOLAA group chat
 Alzbeta: *Girls, help.*

For a second I stop typing. Am I being dramatic? More footsteps. Nope. Definitely not dramatic.

MIOLAA group chat
 Alzbeta: *Call cops now, I'm home!*

No more noise is coming from upstairs. Should I just stay here? I could call the cops myself, but what if I get distracted? I need to stay focused. I know I can count on the girls.

The TV in my bedroom is turned on. I scream, even louder than last time. It feels good in a way, letting out all this tension that's stuck in my body. That damn video again. This time, I'm ranting about the humidity in Singapore. That's it. I'm out of here. There's no way I am going up the third floor when I should be going downstairs. I unlock and push the door of my parents' bedroom open and rush down the stairway. I notice the footsteps above me getting louder and faster. Not today; this is not happening today.

As I arrive at the entrance, I run to the main gate. It's locked. I used the key just a moment ago to let Matej out. *Where is it?* I fumble around for the keys, but I can't find them in any of my pockets. Great. They must've dropped out of my trousers when I bent down for the remote.

Maybe I should run back upstairs and check the entertainment room and my parents' bedroom. They could also just be lying on the table in the living room. Then I hear it again—the creaking floorboards. It raises all the hairs on the back of my neck. This can't be Matej.

I quickly look behind me. I notice someone is walking down the stairway from the second floor. Black boots. A long, old dark blue overcoat. I can practically smell it. There is something stoic, almost regal about the way this figure is walking down the stairs. I sense no hesitance whatsoever in the way he carries himself. My stomach tenses up as I notice he is holding a giant butcher's knife. This figure knows what he wants, and I'm afraid I'm about to find out what that really means. Before I can make out his face, I decide to make a run for it towards the veranda.

I run past the living room, quickly scanning the room for keys. *Nothing.* I up my pace and go to the veranda. I can hear the figure has reached the entry hall. I look up and notice the dark shadows are still dancing on the glass ceiling, almost mockingly. The stained-glass doors of the veranda aren't locked. I thought I had locked them earlier today. No time—I need to get the hell out of here.

Just as I open the doors of the veranda that lead out to the forest, I get a text message.

Unknown Number: *MIOLA.*

*What? Who is this? What does the group chat have to do with all of*

## CHAPTER 46

*this?*

Right then, I feel it—this dark figure walking towards me, looking at me. The slowest pace. A part of me really wants to look back, but I have never been this scared in my life. I am completely frozen. I know I need to run, but—

He grabs my left hand. I let out the most intense scream I've ever screamed. I feel nothing. Then it comes rushing in all at once, the pain. As if woken from a dream I look at my hand and see the blood. I don't know how many seconds I stand there, looking at the stab wound in my left hand, looking up at this dark looming figure. *Could this be him?*

I instinctively kick the figure in the groin. Not waiting for a reaction, I slam the glass door into his face and run into the forest. I wonder if I actually hurt or even killed him. I did hear the glass door smashing. I need to get out of here. The neighbours. I see a light at the opposite side of the forest. That must be the Breinsteins.

I get another text. Startled, I stand still and take my mobile, trying to ignore the pain in my hand.

Matej: *What's going on? The girls are worried!*

Then I hear it: the soggy, wet leaves of the forest being walked on. The figure is right behind me; I can feel him breathing down my neck. I look back and scream as loud as I can. "David! Julia!" I run through the gloomy, muddy forest towards the Breinsteins'. At this time in the evening, the forest always looks mysterious and Gothic. Just dark, majestic branches looming over the city, hiding more stories than any of us want to discover. The figure is still after me, but he seems to be losing speed. I sprint as fast as I possibly can, past these massive trees and little ponds. I can barely see anything in this darkness—the wet branches keep hitting my face. The soil feels slippery, but I do the best I can. Just keep moving, straight on. Tree past tree. I can see their porch light; I'm getting closer. All of a sudden, my knees twist a bit, and my feet feel wet. I stumble. It takes me a moment to realise I have fallen down in one of the ponds. Luckily it isn't too deep, but I am still shivering from the ice-cold water. The stench of the rotten leaves in the pond makes me want to vomit.

I pull myself out of the pond and frantically look around me. Nobody. All I see is my own breath, like a misty grey cloud against the black outlines of the trees. Maybe I made it out safely. Maybe I outran him. He probably doesn't know the ins and outs of this forest the way I do. I just need to get to the neighbours' house and call the police.

A sudden sharp pain stabs my lower back. I drop down. As I try to breathe, I notice I cough up a bit of blood. It tastes like metal, like dirty old metal.

"Please, don't hurt me! I'll do anything!"

The tall, strong figure lifts me up. He looks straight into my eyes. Is that a mask? I notice the fiery eyes staring back at me. They look familiar, or at least I think they do. So much pain. The metal taste lingers in my mouth. He pushes me back down to the ground as if he wants me to make it out alive. Or, as if he's playing with me, toying with me. I get up from the soggy ground and try to run, but I'm not sure where I'm running to. My vision is getting blurry. *Is that them? Am I getting closer?*

Another stab. This time in my left leg. He seems to have hit a nerve, as the pain shoots up right to my head. An intense pressure pounds my forehead. I am not sure if I am still screaming or if the screaming is going on inside my head. I

## CHAPTER 46

need to make it to the Breinsteins'. A bit further. I hear them — I can hear them. I'm sure it's Julia.

"Alzy? Alzbeta, oh my God, what is -? David, call the police!"

It's them; I've made it. Although my vision is horribly blurred, I can still tell Julia is running towards me. Sweet relief. I take a moment to breathe a bit deeper as I try to ignore all the pain I am in. My knees are shaky, but I am still here. David stands on his front porch, a bit frozen, on his phone with the police. I can tell by his body language that he is far from the usual cool, collected guy right now.

"Julia, help me! I'm being—" I look back at the dark forest behind me, but it's gone quiet again.

"I'm right here, honey, you'll be fine! David is calling the police. They will catch whoever did this to you."

"Can't you see him? I have no idea who—"

"Save your breath, Alzbeta. We will get you inside. I'll make you a nice cup of chamomile tea, and we will stay with you until your parents come home."

All of a sudden, Julia screams , "Behind you: watch out!"

The figure appears from behind the tree next to me. I feel a knife slicing through my spine, cutting through all the veins and bones. I hear Julia shrieking. I can't see her anymore, though. I can't see anything. I can't feel anything.

## About the Author

As someone who grew up in the 80s and 90s, Alan Shivers fell in love with the campy, MTV-era type of slashers. He mixes these 80s and 90s Slashers with modern European vibes in his trilogy Europea Halls and his novel The Namaste Slasher.

Next to his love for slashers and all things horror, Alan loves architecture, his Romanian stray dog, meditation and learning different languages.

He is based in Brussels, Belgium.

**SOCIAL MEDIA:**

Instagram: AlanShiversAuthor
TikTok: AlanShiversAuthor
Facebook: Alan Shivers Author

I have also set up a Facebook group about **Queer Horror Books**. Join our community here:
https://www.facebook.com/share/imfy1BLWuST1EQ7D/

**TRIGGER WARNING:**

As this is a Slasher Novel, there are many scenes full of violence, blood, gore and descriptions of deceased people. The book gets quite tense, which might be too intense for sensitive readers.

There are implicit mentions of Sexual, Physical, and Mental Abuse.

There are scenes of Cannibalism.

Viewer discretion is advised.

**Subscribe to my newsletter:**

✉ https://mailchi.mp/b57ece14816e/europea-halls-trilogy

# Also by Alan Shivers

Did you enjoy "The Namaste Slasher"? Then definitely give my Slasher Trilogy "Europea Halls" a go!

**Europea Halls**

Welcome to Europea Halls. Only the select few have made it into these prestigious dorms in the capital of the EU, Brussels.

When six best teenage friends get stalked by a serial killer, the campus is on high alert. As the body count piles up, it seems the killer knows a thing or two about slasher movies. Can these girls fight back in time to discover the truth behind the gruesome murders, or will no-one live to tell the tale?

A Slasher Novel inspired by 90s Slasher Movies such as "Scream", "I Know What You Did Last Summer" and "Urban Legend" with a modern European twist.

Who will the Final Girl be or have the rules changed this time around?

**Europea Halls 2: A Summer in Budapest**
When the survivors of Europea Halls' massacre go on a summer trip to Budapest, they are in dire need of a good time. However, when one of their new friends gets brutally killed, it seems like the past is still hunting them.

Will the group be able to crack the code on how to bend the rules of a sequel or is the killer one step ahead of them?

**Europea Halls 3**
When the survivors of the summer massacre in Budapest are forced to go to Brussels, they will learn the hard way that the final chapter of a Slasher Trilogy always goes back to the beginning.

Printed in Great Britain
by Amazon